Have Yourself a Merry Little Christmas

MERRY FARMER

HAVE YOURSELF A MERRY LITTLE CHRISTMAS

Click here for a complete list of other works by Merry Farmer.

If you'd like to be the first to learn about when the next books in the series come out and more, please sign up for my newsletter here: http://eepurl.com/RQ-KX

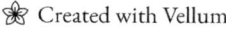 Created with Vellum

Chapter One

The very last thing Miss Charlotte Sloane had expected from her Christmas holidays was to spend them in the tiny island kingdom of Aegiria. Nor would she have expected to be there as the particular guest of her dearest friend, Lady Priya Rathborne-Paxton, Countess Cathraiche, mere weeks after Priya's marriage to Francis Rathborne-Paxton, Lord Cathraiche. Priya was surprised to be spending her honeymoon in Aegiria as well, as she explained to Charlotte when the hasty invitation was issued, just a fortnight before. But after the discovery that Prince Petrus of Aegiria was the secret love child of the Marquess of Vegas, father of the Rathborne-Paxton brothers, and therefore Lord Cathraiche's half-brother, the decision was made that the entire family, all four brothers and their new wives, would travel to Aegiria to reconcile with their surprise sibling.

There was, however, another reason entirely that Charlotte was devilishly excited to be included in the family holiday. One that Priya knew about, but that few others were privy to. And that was her very special acquaintance with Prince Petrus himself. The two had met when Charlotte had invited Priya to spend a holiday in Brighton with her family over the summer. She and Priya had met Petrus at the train station. Over the next few days, Charlotte and Petrus had developed a friendship. That friendship had continued through correspondence ever since, though even Priya did not know about the content of the sweet letters that had been exchanged.

Petrus had hinted an invitation to Aegiria might be in Charlotte's future a month ago. He'd hinted that quite a few other things might be in Charlotte's future as well, if his family should approve.

Which was why Charlotte was breathless and bright with anticipation as the ferry carrying the entire Rathborne-Paxton party from Copenhagen and across the Baltic Sea to Solrighavn, the main city—the only true city on the island of Aegiria—approached the harbor.

"I was not entirely certain that Aegiria actually existed," Charlotte said, leaning out over the railing near the front of the ferry, one gloved hand on her hat to keep it from being blown off, as if leaning might bring her to her destination sooner. "It has always seemed rather like a fairy tale kingdom to me."

Priya laughed at her side, though Charlotte noticed her friend had one hand clasped on the back of Charlotte's coat, as if she could prevent Charlotte from falling into the sea. "It *is* rather like a fairy tale kingdom," she said. "As I understand it, Aegiria is like a world unto itself."

"It was part of the Kingdom of Denmark for quite some time in the Middle Ages," Lord Cathraiche said as he walked up to join Charlotte and Priya at the railing. "At least, until King Magnus the first was granted the entire island as his own sovereign territory after services to the King of Denmark in one of their many wars with Sweden in the thirteen hundreds. Sweden tried to take it a few times, but they never succeeded. The Aegirian Navy has always been first-rate."

Charlotte wasn't certain she cared about the Aegirian Navy. Unless, that was, Prince Petrus had served in it and had stories to tell of daring dos at sea.

Charlotte was much more interested in certain domestic laws of the fascinating island kingdom.

"There are quite a great many princes in Aegiria," she said, half a statement of the things Petrus had written to her and half the things she'd discovered through her own research. "Any member of the royal family has the right to call themselves a prince. And inheritance is determined by the female line instead of the male, which I find utterly remarkable."

"Royal inheritance passes through the female line?" Alice, Mr. Samuel Rathborne-Paxton's wife, a woman who had quickly become Charlotte's friend in the last few weeks, as plans for the holiday voyage were made, asked in her lilting, Irish accent. She stepped over to join the rest of them at the rail, her son, Ryan, with her. Ryan seemed more interested in the action of the boatmen and the men on shore as the ferry was drawn in and moored against a dock than the conversation of adults.

Charlotte hummed and nodded to Alice. "King Magnus the first insisted on it. The legend goes that he was so deeply enamored of his wife, Queen Petronella, that he made it law that her sons and daughters and her descendants through the female line would be the ones to inherit the kingdom."

"Sounds more like Queen Petronella had her husband wrapped around her little finger and could bend a king to her will," Samuel said, stepping up behind Alice and wrapping his arms around her. As shockingly inappropriate as the gesture was, Samuel kissed his wife's cheek as he held her in his arms and said, "Which is a state of being that I approve of entirely."

Alice laughed aloud. "If you ask me, it sounds as though some clever woman hundreds of years ago realized that you will always know the maternity of a child, but you can never be certain about the paternity."

Charlotte noted the way Samuel laughed low in his throat and shifted one of his hands to Alice's belly. She caught her breath and smiled. Perhaps there would be a Christmas announcement from Alice and Samuel to go with the holiday cheer of reuniting the family with Petrus.

Lord Cathraiche was either unaware of his brother and sister-in-law's affection or felt he needed to distract from it. "Inheritance through the female line is the reason Petrus is a Prince of Aegiria instead of merely being my father's bastard. Begging your pardon, Miss Sloane," he added with a bashful nod for Charlotte.

"I don't mind the use of rough language," Charlotte laughed. "My father was born middle class, and there are times when I suspect my mother was snatched up from an even lower order than that. Such language is, sadly, commonplace in our household." She peeked at Alice and Samuel. "As is a certain unguarded level of affection."

In fact, her father and mother were so lax in propriety around the children that Charlotte knew full well why she had so many brothers and sisters. She desperately feared that she'd heard several of the youngest ones conceived through the walls of their family's crowded house. She was not an ignorant miss with no understanding of such things.

Lord Cathraiche cleared his throat and continued with his explanations. "Petrus's mother, Princess Dagmar, is the sister of King Milas, and even though he was born before she married Lord Hektor, under Aegirian law, Petrus is still considered a member of the royal family and, as such, has the right to be called a prince."

"He cannot inherit any of the family's property or carry

out any official duties," Charlotte picked up the explanation from what Petrus had explained to her. "Then again, he is only the nephew of the king and not one of his several sons, so he would not be in line to inherit anything anyhow. Petrus is quite happy to make his own fortune and find a place for himself in life, which is why he has been so interested in learning the sort of business that my father is in."

Several sets of surprised eyes turned to Charlotte. Charlotte's face heated. While Priya knew that she and Petrus had been corresponding, Charlotte hadn't revealed the depths of the attachment the two of them had developed through their letters.

Lord Cathraiche seemed to catch on. He nodded slowly, a smile lighting his eyes, even though he kept his mouth straight. "Indeed," he said. "Petrus is quite industrious. He is well thought of by the royal family as well. His is quite close with his cousins, the other princes and princesses, and he has both a younger brother, Prince Fredrik, and a sister, Princess Brigitta, who were sired by Lord Hektor."

"Petrus considers Lord Hektor like his own father," Charlotte said as the ferry bumped hard against the dock, signaling their arrival at last. When she received another round of stares of awe, she cleared her throat, feeling her face heat as if she'd given away too much, and said, "Lord Hektor is a lovely man, as I understand it. Any man who would fall in love with Princess Dagmar after she had already borne a child out of wedlock must be a wonderful person."

"Morals and customs in Aegiria are much more liberal than in England," Lord Cathraiche agreed. "The place of women especially has been higher than most other kingdoms, ever since King Magnus established the rules. And while Aegiria has remained small and insular, I believe it is a model of how the equality of women is not such a bad thing."

Charlotte was glad to hear Lord Cathraiche say as much.

She was glad her friend had married a man who was so generous in his outlook about women. It was a great deal different from the way Priya had been raised in Koch Bihar.

Their conversation was brought to an end out of necessity as the ferry was secured and the family prepared to debark. Several of the Rahtborne-Paxton family servants had come along for the holiday, and Petrus had sent a few servants from the Aegirian palace to attend to them all and show them the way.

As they stepped off the ferry and onto the bustling dock along Solrighavn's waterfront, excitement swooped through Charlotte's insides. It had been months since she'd seen Petrus in London. Those months felt like years to her. Petrus had been in London for a short time in November, but Charlotte had been away in Bristol with her family, attending the hasty wedding of a cousin—who apparently had as few scruples as her parents did when it came to relations between the sexes, considering the loose fit of her wedding gown.

She glanced around for Petrus now, her skin prickling in anticipation of seeing the man who had made her understand why her kin had such relaxed morals. Of course, she and Petrus had never done anything more than smile heatedly at each other while waltzing, but Charlotte was the first to admit she would not mind throwing caution to the wind, if the opportunity presented itself. She was well aware that her Christmas might involve a proposal, after all, so what point was there in delaying the inevitable.

"Lord Cathraiche, welcome."

They were met at the end of the dock by a handsome, middle-aged man dressed in royal livery so fine it could have been a fashionable suit.

"Mr. Valentin?" Lord Cathraiche asked, approaching the man with a hopeful smile.

"At your service, my lord," the man bowed. "King Milas

has sent me to greet you and to bring you to the palace directly. If you would care to follow me."

Their entire party was quite a sight as they made their way up a slight hill from the dock and through quaint, stone buildings with red slate roofs. The entire Rathborne-Paxton clan, when taken together, was a mish-mash of colorful personalities and liveliness. Since the departure of Lord Vegas, the odious patriarch, to India in the fall, and following the colorful, if not always society-approved marriages of the brothers, the Rathborne-Paxton family had become a happy one. In Charlotte's experience, they were all quite chatty when they were together, as was the case on their short journey from the dock to the palace. The journey was so short that they walked instead of taking a carriage, though Charlotte spotted a wagon gathering their baggage on the dock.

"The buildings are so beautiful," Alice commented, escorted by Samuel on one side and holding Ryan's hand on the other. "The way they've painted the fronts in such bright colors makes for a cheery sight."

"It might even be enough to keep people happy through long, cold, possibly rainy winters," Ellen said as Joseph helped her up a small flight of stone stairs.

"Is there a theater in Aegiria?" Nan asked, gripping Dean's hand tightly as she glanced in every direction as they made their way down a wide, festively decorated thoroughfare lined with shops.

"Indeed, madam," Mr. Valentin said as he led them all. "Aegiria has a long tradition of supporting the arts in all their forms."

"I dare say they might like some sort of a production headlined by the famous—or perhaps now infamous—Nanette D'Argent," Dean told his wife with a low laugh.

Their flirting continued, but Charlotte barely noticed it. She was too engaged in staring at the adorable shops and carts that lined the main road to the palace. She might have only heard about Aegiria recently, but the kingdom appeared to be thriving and peaceful, whether it was well-known or not. The shops they passed were filled with everything from embroidery to leather goods. They passed bakeries with displays of curled buns in their windows, and pie shops from which delicious scents rose up.

As they approached the end of the street—which seemed to open into an attractive square that could easily be the site of formal gatherings or proclamations—and the gates of the palace beyond, Charlotte noted that nearly every building had very specific bundles of holy, ivy, and intricately woven wheat stalks hanging above their doorways.

"What is the significance of the bundles of greenery over the doors?" she asked Mr. Valentin.

Mr. Valentin turned to her with a smile. "They are a Christmas tradition in Aegiria," he explained. "Every house and shop creates their own unique design. The bundles hang over the doorways until Christmas Eve, when the royal family hosts a traditional ball. At the midpoint of the ball, a Christmas Princess is chosen from the guests, and all the bundles are presented to her as a sign of the love and loyalty of the Aegirian people."

"Who ends up chosen as the Christmas Princess?" Nan asked, her face lighting up, as if she might enjoy the title.

"It can be anyone," Mr. Valentin explained. "That is the point of it. The Christmas Princess could be a royal or a commoner. She could be someone whose family roots extend back into the mists of Aegiria's past, or she could be a newcomer who stepped off the boat yesterday." He smiled teasingly at Charlotte as he spoke.

Charlotte returned that smile fourfold. She liked that even a royal steward from the palace could joke with a woman like her. It spoke well of the attitude of the entire royal family.

Mr. Valentin showed them all into the palace, and once again, Charlotte found herself searching in every direction for a sign of Petrus. He wasn't in the courtyard between the gate and the palace itself, although several brightly painted carriages were arranged as if on display. He wasn't in the impressive front foyer either.

Charlotte glanced around that amazing room with as much awe as any of the Rathborne-Paxtons. And with good reason. The front hall—and, Charlotte assumed, the entire palace—was a magnificent blend of old and new. Everywhere she looked, the architecture was of a style that made her think of medieval splendor, perhaps even Viking glory. At the same time, the palace held a great deal of modern furnishings, and the air was neither too cold—due to a lack of fireplaces—nor too thick and stuffy.

"Lord Cathraiche?"

They all turned to find a beautiful woman just beyond her middle years approaching them. She wore a day gown in a style that would have made designers in Paris jealous, but her grey hair was tied up in braids that more closely resembled drawings Charlotte had seen of Scandinavian peasants.

"Welcome to Aegiria," the woman greeted them all, coming to meet them with a bright smile.

"Your majesty," Lord Cathraiche said, bowing deeply to the woman.

Charlotte, along with the rest of the Rathborne-Paxtons, gasped and dropped into curtsies and bows. She didn't know how Lord Cathraiche knew Queen Sylvia, or how he had recognized the woman so quickly. Queens did not generally greet their guests in the foyer of their castles, or so Charlotte believed. She supposed it made perfect sense, considering what she knew of Aegiria, but it was still a surprise.

"What a lovely group you all make," Queen Sylvia said, smiling broadly at her guests. Like Petrus, the queen spoke

English perfectly, with only a slight, musical accent that was unlike any other Charlotte had ever heard. "We have been expecting you," the queen went on. "Come with me. I will give you a brief tour of the palace, the end of which is a feast that has already been laid out to satisfy our hungry travelers."

"Thank you, your majesty," Lord Cathraiche replied for them all.

Charlotte was filled with warmth, and her excitement doubled as they continued from the foyer to a long hallway that must have run the length of the castle. Queen Sylvia said something to Lord Cathraiche, but Charlotte didn't catch it. She was too busy craning her neck and peeking into every room they passed in search of Petrus.

They passed a great many rooms—parlors, a ballroom, and even a library containing a tall Christmas tree. Part of her wanted to stay back and explore the vast library more, but Petrus was not there. Everything was decorated beautifully, with the same sort of holly, ivy, and braided wheat decorations that had graced the city. Along with those arrangements were what seemed like miles of turquoise and green ribbon. Several shiny baubles were hung from the ribbon as well, giving the entire palace a festive air.

It was all lovely, but with every step Charlotte took, her heart grew more anxious. Petrus was at the palace, was he not? Everything he'd told her was true, wasn't it? He was a beloved member of the royal family and resided at the palace along with the rest of them, was that not right?"

"Here we are," the queen said at last, as they were led into a large but somehow still cozy dining room. "And not only is the feast already laid out, it seems you will have the privilege of meeting one of our other guests for the season as well."

Charlotte pulled her gaze away from staring into the corners of the room, searching for Petrus, to see one of the most beautiful women she'd ever seen coming forward to stand at the queen's side.

"This is Lady Jenny Lindstrom," Queen Sylvia introduced the woman with a bright smile. "She has been our guest these many months now, and we could not do without her."

"How do you do?" Lady Jenny asked, curtsying beautifully and nobly. Charlotte noted that, as lovely as the woman was—with thick, blonde hair, blue eyes, and soft, pink lips—she did not smile. To Charlotte, it seemed almost as though she were a great deal too grand to smile.

"The pleasure is all ours, Lady Jenny," Lord Cathraiche spoke for them all yet again. "Allow me to introduce you to my family."

Charlotte studied Lady Jenny a bit more as Lord Cathraiche introduced everyone. She seemed to be everything Charlotte was not—refined, elegant, and well-mannered. There was a degree of tension around the woman that Charlotte could not put her finger on, though. She didn't think she could come right out and say Lady Jenny was unhappy, but something was...off.

"And this is Miss Charlotte Sloane," Lord Cathraiche finished up the introductions. "She is a dear friend of our family."

"And she is a dear friend of mine."

Charlotte sucked in a breath and whirled around to see Petrus entering the room. The comment had come from him, and it made Charlotte's heart sing. She noticed briefly that Lady Jenny seemed to tense even more at the sight of Petrus, but Charlotte's own heart was too filled with joy to pay it any mind.

There he was, Petrus, her love, in all his regal glory. At last, the two of them could be reunited.

Chapter Two

P etrus had been beside himself for most of the day, ever since one of the palace staff had informed him that the ferry from Copenhagen had been spotted on the horizon and their guests would be with them soon. He was delighted to spend Christmas with not only his mother's family, but the other, new part of his heritage. His newly discovered Rathborne-Paxton half-brothers and their wives were an utter delight, and he felt like a child awaiting the arrival of Santa's sleigh.

But what had had Petrus flitting about from meaningless task to meaningless task just to distract himself from waiting since the moment he'd awoken that morning was the promise that Miss Charlotte Sloane would be with his half-family.

"She really is the most remarkable woman," he told his younger brother, Fredrik, as he paced the length of the sitting room they shared in their mother's wing of the palace.

"So you've told me a hundred times at least already," Fredrik said with a lopsided grin as he glanced up from the newspaper he was reading in his chair by the fireplace.

Petrus sent him a flat look to say he knew Fredrik was

teasing him, then went on. "Her father is a successful industrialist and shipping magnate. I admire everything he has done and the successes he has had through doing it. His outlook on business and trade is almost American, it is so progressive. He has earned his fortune several times over."

"Did you not say he was born in the middle classes, though?" Fredrik asked.

"He was," Petrus nodded, pacing past the window and looking out over the sea yet again. "That is why the Sloane family is only grudgingly accepted in polite society in London."

"I always did find the British to be a bit too devoted to class and class divides," Fredrik said, turning a page of his newspaper. "A man is a man, no matter what his status at birth. And a man who started with nothing and has become wealthy should be admired even more, not shunned because he has no title, or because everything he has did not belong to his father first."

A sharp, humorless laugh sounded from the parlor's doorway, and both Petrus and Fredrik turned to see their cousin Oskar entering the room.

"Spoken like a true Aegirian," Oskar said. His face was set in the same frown he'd been wearing all too often as of late.

Oskar was the crown prince and heir to the throne, but no one would have known it from the way he had seemed dissatisfied about life in the last year or so. The change in his cousin's personality had been so noticeable that Petrus felt guilty about spending so much time in England, away from the palace. He and Oskar had been close for their whole lives, and he should have been there for his cousin.

Fredrik stood, folded the newspaper, and set it aside. "I am proud of our kingdom's progressive ways," he said with a shrug. "Nowhere in the world will you find ideals of equality and equanimity like we have in Aegiria."

"Yes, which is perhaps why so many of our neighbors fear us and seek to keep us as quiet and insignificant as possible," Oskar said, walking over to join Petrus, as if he would pace along with him. "There are days when I feel as though the only thing keeping Sweden or Germany from invading and annexing us is our insignificant size."

Petrus laughed despite the seriousness of the statement. "My dear Oskar," he said. "Always the diplomat and future king."

"Someone needs to be concerned about Aegiria's place in the world," Oskar defended himself. "Our way of life depends on being sovereign and independent."

"Which we will always be as long as we maintain our status as every nation in Europe's best friend," Fredrik said. He walked over to clap a hand on Oskar's shoulder and said, "No one will invade Aegiria. Few people even know we're here."

"And I'm certain you will seek to keep it that way," Petrus laughed.

Oskar sent Petrus a frown, then said, "Speaking of people being here, your guests from England have just arrived."

Petrus's heart leapt immediately to his throat, pounding away as if it longed to jump from his body and rush straight to Charlotte.

"Then why are we lollygagging around here?" Petrus asked, making straight for the door.

The moment had come, and wild horses couldn't keep him away from his sweetheart. And he absolutely considered Charlotte to be his sweetheart, despite the fact she was English and lived so far away. From the moment he'd met her in Brighton, he'd known that she was the only woman for him.

Which was more of a problem than he wanted to admit.

"Petrus, hold up a moment," Oskar called after him.

Petrus clenched his jaw and slowed his steps, turning back to wait for Oskar and Fredrik to catch up with him in the hall.

Oskar wore his customary frown, but it seemed somehow more pronounced.

"We must talk," Oskar said, falling into step with Petrus, Fredrik walking on Petrus's other side, and setting a sedate pace.

Petrus didn't like the serious set of Oskar's expression. He had a bad idea he knew what Oskar wanted to talk about.

"It is all well and good that you made yourself a friend in Miss Sloane, whose arrival I know you have been anticipating even more than the Rathborne-Paxton family's," Oskar said, "but you know full well that Father has other plans for you."

Petrus tried not to stumble as they reached the stairs and headed down to the main part of the palace. He knew too well what his cousin meant.

"With all due respect to Uncle Milas," Petrus said, "I should be at liberty to choose my own bride."

Both Oskar and Fredrik tensed by Petrus's sides as they reached the ground floor and continued on.

Oskar cleared his throat and, keeping his voice low as they walked through a part of the palace filled with servants and palace retainers, said, "Lady Jenny Lindstrom has been sent all the way from Stockholm for you. She is a fine and noble woman. It is not right for you to throw her over in this manner, simply because some wealthy Englishwoman has snagged your attention instead."

The words felt like ice water being poured down Petrus's back. He had been aware from the moment Lady Jenny was introduced to him that both his family and hers expected things from them. Lady Jenny had arrived just as he was about to depart for England on his first voyage to search for his half-brothers, and he hadn't had much time to speak to her. Then he'd met Charlotte.

In every way, Lady Jenny and the whispered claim she had to him should have taken precedence over Charlotte. Their acquaintance was longer, Lady Jenny's position in the Swedish aristocracy meant she outranked Charlotte, and the king himself had expectations of the match. But Petrus's heart was already spoken for.

He just wasn't certain that was enough, or that he could delay the inevitable any longer.

All of those troublesome thoughts were blasted from his mind the moment he stepped into the large dining room where luncheon had been set. There she was, amidst the bustle and noise of his half-brothers and their wives, looking as sweet and radiant as Petrus remembered her to be.

"Char—er, Miss Sloane," Petrus said, tripping over his tongue and threatening to trip over his own feet as he swept into the dining room, heading toward his sweetheart.

Charlotte brightened like the Aurora Borealis at the sight of him, which warmed Petrus's heart. She truly did look perfect in a dove-gray traveling coat, the hem of her cranberry-red skirt showing below the hem. Charlotte's abundant, soft hair was caught up in the latest style...in a way that made Petrus want to run his fingers through it and ruin the style until Charlotte's hair fell in golden waves around her shoulders. Charlotte's blue eyes were bright, and her cheeks rosy from fresh air and travel. She was simply the most beautiful, the most perfect—

The sound of Oskar clearing his throat snapped Petrus out of his thoughts.

"Won't you introduce us to your friends?" Oskar asked.

Aegiria might have been a progressive enigma, but certain rules of society still applied, and Petrus was in danger of breaking all of them.

He reined himself in and turned his attention from Charlotte—who lowered her eyes with an understanding half-smile —and strode over to shake Francis's hand.

"It is good to see you, my friend," he greeted his half-brother. "I trust your voyage was easy?"

"It was indeed," Francis said. He peeked between Petrus and Charlotte, as if he knew which way the wind was blowing.

Petrus moved to stand by Francis's side, facing Oskar and Fredrik. "I would like you to meet Lord Francis Rathborne-Paxton, Earl of Cathraiche," he said, then continued quickly with, "And his wife, Lady Priya. And this is my cousin, Crown Prince Oskar of Aegiria, and my brother, Prince Fredrik."

"How do you do," Francis said, bowing respectfully to both Oskar and Fredrik.

The next several minutes were spent in what felt like endless introductions as each of the Rathborne-Paxton brothers and their wives were introduced, hands were shook, and bows and curtsies made. Petrus was aware of Lady Jenny standing at the fringes of the assembly with Queen Sylvia, and also that more and more of the royal family, including Oskar's siblings, were making their way into the room, adding to the necessary introductions.

It felt like ages before he was able to work his way around to Charlotte's side so that he could introduce her. "And last but very much not least, this is Miss Charlotte Sloane."

He smiled at Charlotte with a fondness that anyone in the room would have a hard time mistaking.

Which was, unfortunately, quite literally the case. A kind of hush fell over the now crowded room as the Aegirian folk all studied Charlotte with particular curiosity. The Aegirian folk *and* Lady Jenny.

Lady Jenny, whose face pinched slightly in distress, and who clutched her hands together in front of her stomach as though her world stood on the verge of crumbling apart.

A worrying twist of guilt and confusion racked Petrus. He wasn't certain what to do. He was loath to offend or slight Lady Jenny, or anyone else, but it had been so terribly long since he'd seen Charlotte and since he'd been close enough to touch her.

"Thank you for the kind introduction, Prince Petrus," Charlotte said, somehow maintaining a greater degree of decorum than he felt capable of in the moment. She turned to the rest of the family—which numbered over a dozen by that point—smiled, and bobbed a short curtsy. "It is such an honor and a pleasure to meet you all, particularly as I am but a stranger in your midst. Your kindness and your hospitality touch me."

The entire family seemed to breathe a sigh of relief as they moved about the table to take their seats. Petrus could have kissed Charlotte right then and there. She might have been born to an odd sort of people, but she had learned deportment somewhere, and it was serving her well.

"Shall we all enjoy this delightful meal our kitchens have concocted?" the queen asked. It was a thinly disguised order for everyone to sit and eat.

"Yes, Mother, I think that is an excellent idea," Oskar said, moving around the edge of the table. "Petrus?" Oskar issued another sort of order with his eyes, jerking his head to the chair beside where Lady Jenny stood, waiting for someone to help her to her seat.

Distress pulsed through Petrus. He smiled to Oskar and Lady Jenny, then shifted quickly to face Charlotte.

"I am so very happy to see you, Charlotte," he whispered. As subtly as he could, he reached toward her, brushing the back of her gloved hand with his fingertips. "We must find a time as soon as possible to speak. In private," he added, leaning even closer to her.

"Yes, indeed," Charlotte whispered back to him, glancing up and meeting his gaze with a mischievous look of her own. "I quite understand your family duties."

Petrus let out a breath of relief. He was more grateful than he could say that Charlotte wasn't the jealous type, and that she seemed to truly understand the obligations he had.

Again, he was tempted to kiss her, but that was impossible. The best he could manage was a small wink that he hoped was concealed before he stepped away.

By the time he made it to the other side of the table, Oskar had already pulled out a chair for Lady Jenny and helped her to sit. He had leaned over Lady Jenny's shoulder so that he could help slide her chair in, and as he straightened, he glared at Petrus. Petrus could hear his indignation over the way Lady Jenny had been slighted in favor of an Englishwoman Oskar didn't know.

Petrus did his best to smile placatingly at Oskar as they took the seats on either side of Lady Jenny, then engaged in light conversation as the servants swooped in to serve the meal.

It was a pleasant meal, all things considered. Their English guests were the focus of conversation as the Aegirian folks asked about everything from their journey to their situations in England. There was much to talk about as well, since it was apparent from the start that the Rathborne-Paxton brides were all unique in their own ways. Petrus's cousin, Princess Luna, knew Nanette D'Argent and had seen her in a play on her last trip to London. Once that was revealed, the conversation steered toward theatrical topics, which led to discussion of the Christmas ball that would take place in the palace on Christmas Eve.

"Everyone—from Father to the boys who sweep the streets—is invited to participate in some way," Luna told their guests, her face alight with excitement, since the ball was only a week away.

"Not everyone fits in the palace ballroom, of course," Petrus's sister, Brigitta, picked up the explanation, "but we allow anyone who would like to participate to come into the palace grounds."

"We decorate the palace from head to toe for the occasion," Luna continued. "It is our family tradition. I do hope you will help us with the decorations."

"The royal family decorates their own house?" Priya asked with a blink of surprise.

"It is unusual, I know," Princess Luna said, "but it is symbolic of the obligation Aegirian rulers have to their subjects."

"That sounds like a lovely tradition," Ellen, Joseph's new bride, said in her slightly too loud American accent. "I'd be willing to help."

"As would I," Alice added with a smile, halfway through cutting the meat on her son's plate.

"We should make some sort of game of it," Luna said, glancing down to her brother, Lars, and sister, Freya. "We have a few family games already."

"I hope you will participate as well, Miss Sloane," Brigitta said, sending a knowing glance between Petrus and Charlotte.

"I would be delighted," Charlotte said, smiling across the table to Brigitta.

Petrus didn't know much about women, but he could see that something in Charlotte liked the look of Brigitta right away, and vice versa, and that the two of them were set to become the best of friends.

Which was deeply worrying, in a way.

"I do hope you will allow Lady Jenny to participate as well," Oskar said, a bit of a hard edge to his voice.

Shame immediately spilled through Petrus. Even though she was seated right beside him, Lady Jenny had remained so quiet and so small throughout the entire conversation that he'd hardly noticed her. It was terrible manners on his part.

"Yes, of course," he said, struggling to make up for ignoring her...while trying not to put Charlotte off as well.

"Would you like to participate in whatever decorating my sisters and our guests concoct, Lady Jenny?"

Lady Jenny looked as though she had been handed a difficult decision. She peeked at Petrus, then darted a glance across the table to Charlotte, then down to Brigitta and Oskar and some of the others.

Finally, she took in a short breath and said, "Yes, please. That would be delightful."

Her tone suggested anything but delight. In fact, if Petrus hadn't known better, he would have said Lady Jenny was miserable.

"Does Aegiria have a tradition of erecting Christmas trees?" Dean Rathborne-Paxton asked from the other side of the table, his voice perhaps a bit too loud.

Samuel snorted for no apparent reason...except perhaps that his brother had emphasized the word "erecting" a bit too significantly.

It was silly and childish, well beneath the dignity of a noble family like the Rathborne-Paxtons, and the royal family, but the comment did exactly as Petrus figured it was meant to by diverting everyone's attention from the awkward exchange around Lady Jenny.

"Aegiria has decorated for the Christmas season with pine trees long before the rest of the world, Mr. Rathborne-Paxton," Aunt Sylvia herself answered, commanding the attention of everyone at the table. "In fact, I would venture to say that the rest of the world stole the idea from us."

"I'm not so certain about that, Mother," Cousin Viggo, the youngest of Petrus's cousins and the most studious, said. "Traditions of decorating for Yule with pine trees and other greenery dates back hundreds of years."

Petrus was so relieved that his cousin was such a stuffy fount of knowledge that he let out a breath. Lady Jenny turned her head slightly to him at that breath, eyeing him sideways with a deeply worried look. It was enough to snap Petrus straight again and to focus him on his meal.

His anxiety was not helped by the fact that he caught Oskar shifting in his chair and sending him a disapproving look around Lady Jenny. Oskar then offered to serve Lady Jenny from the platter of fish that a servant came by to offer in that moment, glaring at Petrus as if to demonstrate how one was meant to treat a lady who was intended by the family to be his bride.

Petrus felt duly scolded, but he didn't know what to do with the feeling. His attention and his whole heart felt pulled across the table to where Charlotte sat opposite him. Charlotte was doing a much better job of politeness than he was as she smiled and laughed at the appropriate places in the conversation, and ate everything presented to her for lunch, even though Petrus was certain she'd never encountered some of the stranger Aegirian dishes before, like the pickled eel.

It was only when Charlotte sent a quick look across the table, catching his eyes with a knowing look, that Petrus was certain she was deeply aware of him, no matter where her attention appeared to be. He wished the table was narrow enough for him to reach her feet with his under it. He wished the rest of the family was off doing their own thing and that it was just him and Charlotte enjoying the meal. He wished he didn't have a mountain of duty pressing down on his shoulders to complicate what should simply be love.

More than anything, he wished that he would get the chance to speak to Charlotte and to tell her just how much he loved her...before Charlotte heard even the slightest whisper of how he was supposed to engage himself to Lady Jenny as soon as possible.

Chapter Three

Before the end of the day, Charlotte had decided that Aegiria was a beautiful and magical place, and that she wouldn't mind making it her home. Of course, that was putting the cart much too far ahead of the horse, but if the smiles Petrus sent her way as he accompanied the Rathborne-Paxton family on a tour of Aegiria's capital city after lunch was any indication, that particular cart and horse might be united soon.

The royal city was even more beautiful and splendid than the first view Charlotte had of the place walking up from the dock. It was made up of buildings that managed to be both sturdy and beautiful, with quite a few gardens that the residents knew how to plant for optimal color, even though it was December.

The people were some of the friendliest Charlotte had ever encountered. As Petrus explained on his tour—which several of his cousins and his brother and sister had joined them for, along with Lady Jenny—Aegiria was prosperous for its size. The bulk of the island was taken up with farmland and a few small industries, but the wealth of the island kingdom came from their management of the sea. People were content for the most part, and while there were opportunities on the island itself, quite a large percentage of the population went to Europe or the various Scandinavian countries for their education or to work.

The rooms within the palace that Charlotte and her friends were given were splendid as well. Charlotte nearly collapsed into bed that night, after a busy day of travel and forging new friendships. The tradition in Aegiria was to sleep with the windows open at night, even in the cold, under layers of down quilts, nesting in copious amounts of pillows. Charlotte slept like a babe in arms, or perhaps a baby duckling snuggled into its mother's feathers.

By the time Charlotte found herself engaged with various royal family members, decorating one of the parlors for Christmas the next morning, after a hearty breakfast and delightful conversation, there was only one complaint she could think to give. She had not had so much as a spare second alone with Petrus to tell him how delighted she was to see him again, and perhaps to steal the kiss she had dreamed of for so many months now.

"Should these garlands go around the windows or over the fireplace?" she asked Princess Dagmar, Petrus's mother, who was in charge of the decorations for the room where Charlotte worked, along with Priya and Petrus's sister, Brigitta. She held up a fresh, green garland of holly, ivy, and pine that one of the palace servants had brought in earlier.

Princess Dagmar was a handsome woman who had the look of a Viking warrioress, at least, to Charlotte's imagination. She was tall with a strong face and bright eyes that spoke of intelligence and command. Charlotte had no idea how a woman of her obvious presence and power could have fallen for the false charms of the Marquess of Vegas.

"That one goes over the fireplace," Princess Dagmar said with a nod. "These will go over the windows." She crossed to a box of greens and began taking them out and handing them to her daughter and Priya.

"Has the tradition of the family doing their own decorating existed for many years?" Priya asked as she took one of the smaller garlands to a window.

Charlotte could imagine that, for a woman who had been raised to be a rani in the kingdom of Koch Bihar, it must have been strange to do something that was, arguably, servants' work.

"Yes, indeed," Princess Dagmar answered. "The tradition began as a yuletide gift to the servants of the palace, but it extended out to the noble families of Aegiria as well. Now, anyone who owns a household or a business hangs their own Christmas decorations for the servants and those who are employed to enjoy."

"I think I like this Aegirian tradition," Charlotte said, fetching the large pins they were using to fasten the garlands in place around the room. "There is something so equitable about it."

"It has always reminded me of that carol about Good King Wenceslas," Brigitta said, rushing over to hold the other end of Charlotte's garland. "Any royal who serves his or her people is a good example."

Charlotte hummed in agreement as she fastened her end of the garland to the mantel. She liked the Aegirian royals more and more with every passing moment.

"Do the men do similar work?" she asked, hoping she seemed casual when, in fact, she had a specific question in mind. She couldn't hold that question in entirely and blurted out, "Is Petrus off in the palace somewhere, tying bows to balustrades?"

Brigitta laughed, glancing across the room to her mother.

"I would imagine that Prince Petrus is in the ballroom, helping to bring in the trees that have been cut in preparation for the Christmas ball."

There was a knowing light to Brigitta's eyes that Charlotte wouldn't be able to escape. Try as she might to be subtle, she suspected Brigitta already knew about her feelings for Petrus, and hopefully his for her, especially since she'd just slipped up and referred to him informally.

She was about to come right out and ask when Lady Jenny entered the room carrying a large basket of bright red bows.

"The queen has asked me to deliver these to you, and to help, if I can," she said, approaching Princess Dagmar.

Something about Lady Jenny pulled at Charlotte's heart in a way she didn't like. The Swedish noblewoman was beautiful, without a doubt, but she was so...so dour. As if she didn't quite approve of the English invasion that had descended on the palace. Or as if she were unhappy in love somehow.

Charlotte determined right then and there that she would befriend Lady Jenny, whatever it took.

"We could use some of those bows over here, I would think," she said in what she hoped was an inviting voice. She glanced to Brigitta to see if the woman would play along with her plans to draw Lady Jenny in.

Brigitta looked confused for a moment before saying, "Yes, we could use some." She stared at Charlotte in a way that made Charlotte wonder if Petrus's sister knew something she didn't.

Without a word, Lady Jenny brought her basket over to them. She seemed skittish around Charlotte somehow, like she did not want to make friends. Charlotte simply could not imagine what that was all about.

"Why don't we hang the bows together?" she suggested, moving to take the basket from Lady Jenny once her end of the garland was in place.

"I...I should assist Princess Dagmar," Lady Jenny said, glancing over her shoulder to the woman.

"I will help *Mormie*," Brigitta said, skipping away from the fireplace to cross the room to where Princess Dagmar was showing Priya how to arrange the trailing ends of the garland they'd just hung.

Charlotte exchanged a glance with Lady Jenny. She appeared as clueless as Charlotte felt about what to do with being left alone together.

"I've just learned that 'mormie' is the Aegirian diminutive for 'mother'," Charlotte told Lady Jenny in a quiet voice.

"Yes, I know," Lady Jenny said.

Charlotte wanted to pinch her face in disappointment. She felt as though she was not making the best impression on the noblewoman.

"Would you show me how to pin the bows to the garland?" she asked, hoping that deferring to Lady Jenny's wider knowledge and expertise would earn her the woman's friendship.

"It isn't that difficult," Lady Jenny said with just a bit of tartness in her tone. She set the basket down, then took out a bow and used one of the pins to attach it to the garland. "Like this."

"Oh, I see." Charlotte fetched a bow from the basket and pinned it along the garland as well. "Is there a specific pattern, or should we just put them where we see fit?"

Lady Jenny seemed to take an inordinately long time to answer the question. Charlotte hadn't thought it was that complicated. But at last, Lady Jenny let out a long, almost exhausted breath and said, "I do apologize if my manner has seemed curt, Miss Sloane." She bent to take another bow from the basket.

Charlotte's heart leapt for joy. She'd broken through the woman's reserve after all, she just knew it.

"No offense taken," Charlotte said, reaching for a bow herself. "I understand how difficult it must be to spend Christmas so far from one's family, in a foreign country. And please call me Charlotte."

Lady Jenny turned to her with a surprised look…that quickly turned forlorn. "It isn't that, Miss—Charlotte. And thank you for the honor of your name."

Charlotte smiled as she pinned her bow, waiting patiently for Lady Jenny to go on.

Lady Jenny pursed her lips together, worrying her hands in front of her. She then glanced up to meet Charlotte's eyes so quickly that Charlotte nearly sucked in a breath in surprise.

"My father sent me here as a way to strengthen ties between Sweden and Aegiria," she explained in a rush. "It is expected that I will marry into the Aegirian royal family."

"Oh, I see," Charlotte said.

She wasn't a complete stranger to fathers that expected their daughters to marry men of their choosing. Priya had been in nearly that same position, as her father had wished for her to marry a friend of his back in India. More than that. Priya *had* been married to Raja Jogendra Dev Raikut of Jalpaiguri by proxy, though the marriage had been declared invalid by the British courts so that Priya and Lord Cathraiche could wed.

But Lady Jenny's brow furrowed, and she pressed her lips together as though Charlotte didn't understand at all. "I have been in Aegiria for almost a year," she said, "and I have yet to become betrothed."

"I'm certain there is still time," Charlotte said, daring to rest a friendly, comforting hand on Lady Jenny's arm.

Lady Jenny looked alarmed and distressed by the gesture. She met Charlotte's eyes again and said, "That is precisely the problem. There is not time. My father has now told me that if I am not engaged to…to the man he has chosen for me by

Christmas, he will call me home before the new year. And I...I do not wish to leave."

Charlotte nodded slowly as understanding dawned on her. "You wish to stay in Aegiria?" she asked.

Lady Jenny nodded. The poor thing looked near tears.

"I am certain your beloved will propose before Christmas," she said, putting on a smile. "Is not Christmas a time for proposals and romance?"

"It is," Lady Jenny said, "but I fear—"

"Ah, Lady Jenny, there you are," Crown Prince Oskar said as he strode into the doorway.

Lady Jenny leapt away from Charlotte, as if the two of them had been discussing something forbidden.

"I have been asked to fetch you to see if you would help with the trees in the ballroom," Prince Oskar said with a kind, if somewhat tight and guarded smile. Prince Oskar was the only member of the royal family who had seemed offended by Charlotte's presence with his family. He sent her the briefest of looks—one that took the warmth right out of her—then glanced to Lady Jenny again. "My father has requested you join us specifically."

There was something brittle and tight about that final pronouncement, as though it pained Prince Oskar to say those words.

"Yes, your highness," Lady Jenny said with a perfect curtsy.

She left Charlotte's side without another word, though she did glance back at Charlotte with an apologetic look.

The pain in her heart that Lady Jenny gave her—without explanation or reason—deepened as Charlotte watched her leave the room. Something was amiss. Something more than the prospect of Lady Jenny being forced to leave Aegiria. There had to be a reason the woman wanted to stay.

"She is scared of you," Brigitta said, coming back to help as

Charlotte returned to pinning bows to the garland over the fireplace.

"Good heavens," Charlotte exclaimed. "She cannot be. *I* am rather intimidated by *her*."

"You are?" Brigitta frowned curiously at her.

"Indeed," Charlotte said. "For Lady Jenny is clearly a noblewoman of the highest order, whereas I am the daughter of a self-made man. Considering we are in a royal palace, I know which one of us fits and which does not."

"I believe you fit here," Brigitta said, her smile glowing with mischief. "I believe you fit quite well, and that you will continue to fit, if my brother has anything to say about it."

Charlotte's face immediately went hot. "Your brother?" Charlotte's voice cracked with guilt.

Much to her horror, Princess Dagmar and Pryia stepped away from the window where they were working and came over to join them.

"Do not for a moment imagine that I am unfamiliar with the workings of my own son's heart," Princess Dagmar said.

She gestured for Charlotte and Brigitta to join her and Priya at the circle of chairs and the sofa near the center of the room. A platter of special Aegirian Christmas buns sat on a low table there, along with a tea service. Princess Dagmar had evidently decided it was time for the decorators to pause for refreshment.

"I know that my son has met with you several times in London," Princess Dagmar said, pouring tea for Charlotte, then the others. "I know he has written to you quite a bit since then as well."

"You do?" Charlotte asked. She could only imagine what a princess would think of her son falling in love with a commoner.

"I have seen the joy in Petrus's eyes when he reads your

letters, my dear," Princess Dagmar said, smiling with her eyes. "I have seen the delight that you bring him. Now that I have met you in person, I understand that joy and delight entirely."

"How very kind of you to say, Princess Dagmar." Charlotte bowed her head to the woman over her tea.

"I am unsurprised that my eldest son has given his heart away to an Englishwoman," Princess Dagmar continued, handing tea to the others. "He is half English himself, after all."

Charlotte nearly choked on her tea. She knew that the strange laws of Aegiria meant that Petrus was still considered a royal prince, even though he'd been born out of wedlock, but it startled her to hear the matter spoken of so freely.

Princess Dagmar seemed to sense the source of Charlotte's shock.

"I fancied myself in love, my dear," she told Charlotte, as if that were a reason for the openness. "Lord Vegas represented himself falsely to me, to be certain. I was young and in awe of the foreign country I found myself in. I was flattered that a marquess would pay me so much attention. I did not have a friend to caution me as to the man's true intent, and I was led down a dangerous path because of it."

"I...I am very sorry," Charlotte said, at a loss for words.

Princess Dagmar laughed. "I am not," she said, surprising Charlotte. "For even though Petrus was born out of my folly, I do not know what I would do without him."

"That is true," Charlotte said, still stunned for all the ease with which Princess Dagmar told the story.

"More than that," the woman went on, "because of my surprising state, I was too embarrassed to stay for long in this city when I returned from my sojourn in England. I asked to be allowed to stay at the family's summer house in Tjornbay, on the other side of the island. Which is where I met my husband, Hektor. His father is a duke, and he lived on the estate adjoining our family's. We met because I was in self-exile, and his kindness won me over. With Hektor, I have found a love that surpasses description, and I have had two more wonderful children." She reached her hand out to take Brigitta's.

Charlotte smiled at the story, a bit misty-eyed at the romance of it. She wasn't certain what it had to do with her or her correspondence with Petrus, though.

Princess Dagmar seemed to understand her confusion.

"Love can be found in the most unusual of places and with people who would surprise you," she said. "Never mind what others think, what the plans of kings or paupers are." There was a certain something in the way she said that and looked at Brigitta as she did that felt odd to Charlotte, but she went on with, "Follow your heart and let it take you where it would."

"So," Charlotte began, then decided she needed another gulp of tea to fortify herself before going on. "So you approve of my affection for Petrus?" she asked quietly, almost afraid of the answer.

But Princess Dagmar—and Brigitta—smiled widely. "Of course I do," she said. "Because I can clearly see the two of you care for each other. And that is all that matters, not titles or nationalities, or even international diplomacy."

Charlotte was encouraged by those words. She was about to say something more, to ask about Lady Jenny as well, but a sudden, strange squeal from Pryia stopped her.

A moment later, Priya's expression widened with surprise, and she reached behind her to pull a large, ugly Christmas ornament from behind the cushion at her back.

"What in the name of Vishnu's arms is *this*?" she asked, making a face at the hideous thing. It was about the size of a cricket ball, shaped like a boot, and covered with gaudy, black and white sequins.

Princess Dagmar and Brigitta burst into loud laughter so quickly that Charlotte jumped in surprise.

"You've found the boot!" Brigitta proclaimed, clapping her hands and beaming.

"The boot?" Priya arched one eyebrow at Brigitta and handed the ornament to Charlotte.

Charlotte surveyed it with distaste. "What is it?"

Princess Dagmar continued to laugh for a moment before saying, "It is a monstrosity that was given to Princess Luna about ten years ago, when she was a child, by Prince Lars, her twin. She thought it was so ugly that she would only hang it on the back of the family Christmas tree. But every time Lars found it there, he would move it around to the front and center. Then Luna would remove it to the back again, and so on and so forth."

"Until one day when Luna decided enough was enough," Brigitta picked up the story. "She took it off the tree entirely and hid it."

"She didn't have the heart to throw it away completely, you see," Princess Dagmar said. "It was a gift from her twin, after all."

"But Lars found it, of course, and hung it back on the tree," Brigitta said. "And Luna took it off and hid it again."

"It has become a family tradition," Princess Dagmar said, beaming. "Luna hides the boot, and whoever finds it returns it to the Christmas tree. Once it's there, Luna hides it again."

"But if you're caught returning the boot to the tree, whoever catches you can force you to perform a forfeit."

"A forfeit?" Charlotte asked, loving the idea. "What does that entail?"

"Whatever the one who catches you at it wants," Princess Dagmar said. "Two years ago, Prince Leif caught me at it, and

I was forced to sing a tavern song at the supper table that night, in front of everyone."

Charlotte laughed out loud at that. The image of the regal and powerful Princess Dagmar singing a drinking song for her family at supper was a delight.

"I had to walk around wearing a paper crown all day once last year," Brigitta said with a laugh.

"Can anyone play this game or is it for family only?" Priya asked.

"Anyone can play," Brigitta said, sitting straighter, her eyes flashing with mischief. "We've had guests perform some of the most amusing forfeits in the past."

"Then I think Charlotte should attempt to return the boot to the family tree without being caught," Priya said, as mischievous as Brigitta.

"Me?" Charlotte laughed and looked at the boot in her hands.

"Yes," Priya said. "You never know who you might find on your way to return it."

Charlotte caught her breath at the suggestion. Her friend was providing her with a way to find Petrus and have a bit of time alone, so that they might talk. And from the looks on Princess Dagmar's and Brigitta's faces, they liked the plan.

"The family Christmas tree is in the library," Princess Dagmar said. "Go to the end of the hall, then turn right. There's another hall halfway down. Take that to the left and follow it all the way to the end. The library cannot be missed, and the family tree is right in the center of the room."

Charlotte set her teacup aside and glanced at the three women watching her. "Do you think I'll be caught?" she asked, rather hoping she would and that Petrus would catch her. She could only imagine the sort of forfeit he would ask her to pay.

Brigitta shrugged coyly. "There is no way to be sure," she said.

Charlotte wondered if Brigitta would leave to alert her brother as to Charlotte's whereabouts as soon as she left for the library. She could only hope.

"I'll do it," she said, standing and clutching the boot to her stomach. "I'll go right now, and we'll see what happens."

Chapter Four

"A bit to the left," Petrus said as he stood at one end of the palace's vast ballroom, directing a few of the male servants as they erected a Christmas tree. "Mmm, perhaps a bit too much. A little to the right."

The servants adjusted the tree, looking eagerly to him for more instructions.

"Yes, I think that's about right," he said with a smile, then nodded to them. "Fetch the next one, and then that will be the last of them."

"Yes, your highness," the two young men said, bowing to him, then headed off to wherever they'd been bringing the trees in from.

Petrus took a few more steps back to survey the area at that end of the ballroom. A long dais had been set up for the orchestra that would play at the Christmas Eve ball, but it would also be the site of any and all announcements that would be made, including the crowning of the Christmas Princess.

That thought brought an unexpected frown to Petrus's

brow. The selection of the Christmas Princess was not as random as many people believed. The honor usually went to a woman who had performed great acts of kindness during the year, or to a woman who would soon marry into the royal family. It was a means of introducing the bride and giving her warm associations in the hearts of the people of Aegiria.

Petrus knew full well that Lady Jenny was expected to be the Christmas Princess this year. He knew because he was meant to propose to her before Christmas Eve so that the moment could be made perfect and magical.

The problem was that Petrus didn't feel a lick of magic where Lady Jenny was concerned. Friendship and kindness, yes, but not magic. All his feelings of magic were reserved for Charlotte. And what he wouldn't give to see Charlotte step onto the dais wearing the crown of candles and greenery that signaled the Christmas Princess?

"Your highness?"

Petrus jolted out of his soft imaginings of Charlotte standing before everyone, looking resplendent as she was bathed in light, to find Mr. Valentin standing behind him.

"Your highness, Princess Brigitta requested that you go to the library at once," Mr. Valentin went on. "She said she believes the boot is about to be delivered, and she wishes you to have a chance to forfeit its current possessor."

Petrus's face lit into a cheery smile. "Thank you, Valentin."

He hurried off at once, abandoning the decorating work to Fredrik and his cousins. The family's tradition of hiding the Christmas boot was silly in the extreme, but it had also provided some of his fondest memories of Christmases past. He was especially proud of the year when he was fifteen and had caught the king himself returning the boot to the tree. He'd required his uncle to attend their family supper that night wearing his jacket the wrong way around, the buttons running down his back. Everyone had been in stitches as the king strained and pulled at the garment, which was not meant to be worn that way, just to reach his roast and potatoes.

Those thoughts were happily at the front of his mind as he stepped into the library. But instead of finding Brigitta or one of his family members attempting to rehang the hideous boot on the tree—which stood in all its decorated glory in the center of the far wall, between two tall windows that let in sparkling, afternoon light—he found Charlotte studying the tree as if searching for a place to hang the bulky boot ornament she carried.

"Oh!" Charlotte exclaimed, jumping back as though she'd been caught at something wicked, as soon as she spotted Petrus. A moment later, her face burst with joy, and she called out, "Petrus!"

She hung the boot on the nearest bough without much care, then rushed to greet Petrus. Decorum and restraint went out the window the moment Charlotte reached him.

"Charlotte, my darling," he said on a deep sigh of relief. "At last—"

That was as far as he got before Charlotte flung herself at him, throwing her arms around his shoulders and pushing up to her tip-toes so that she could kiss him. Petrus loved that his beloved wasn't shy or reticent about such things. He'd grown up in a palace, where dignity and sophistication were prized traits, but he adored brightness and free expression of affection.

He clasped Charlotte gratefully in his arms, and with as few qualms as it seemed Charlotte had, he kissed her back the way he'd dreamed of kissing her for months now. Their mouths seemed meant for kissing each other, and he was able to part her lips to taste the sweet warmth of her tongue as he slipped his alongside hers.

Charlotte responded with a hum of approval deep in the

back of her throat. The sound sent everything stirring within Petrus, and he adjusted his arms around her to hold her in a way that would scandalize anyone who might come into the room. He wasn't overly concerned with that, though. Almost everyone was busy decorating, which meant the library would be abandoned for most of the day. And even if he was discovered kissing Charlotte and stroking his hands along her sides, brushing one hand over her breast, well, he was a prince of Aegiria. He could get away with such things in his own home.

"I've missed you so much," Charlotte said, pulling back at last, her lips pink from kisses.

"And I have missed you too, my darling," Petrus said, cupping the side of her face and smiling at her as though his heart would burst from his chest. "I hate that we have not had time alone together yet so that I can tell you how much, or so that I can tell you how well you look and how beautiful."

"Petrus." Charlotte spoke his name as though it were a hymn and glanced down, her cheeks shining pink. When she peeked up at him through her long lashes, Petrus's heart caught in his throat, and his trousers went tight. "You look so handsome and regal yourself. And Aegiria is such a beautiful place."

That second statement seemed to fill her with energy. She took a half step back, breaking into an excited smile.

"I never knew such a place existed, but Aegiria is like some sort of dream. Everything is so lovely, and everyone seems so happy. Your family is a delight as well."

"I am rather fond of my family," Petrus said, dropping his hands so that he could hold Charlotte's. "They accept me completely when they do not have to. Many families wouldn't, given the situation."

"And I love that about them," Charlotte said.

Petrus felt a hitch in his chest as he went on. "Not

everyone is completely happy, though," he said, feeling honesty was best. "Aegiria has its share of problems."

Charlotte's brow knit in concern, and she said, "Yes, I've noticed that Lady Jenny is distressed about something."

Petrus's heart skipped a beat. He'd been talking about villagers who weren't satisfied with their crops or young people who found the tiny kingdom too small for their ambitions and who wished to travel abroad. He hadn't been aware that Charlotte knew anything about the situation with Lady Jenny.

He was determined to face that situation immediately and to be as honest as possible about it.

"I know that my uncle expects me to marry the woman for the good of both our kingdoms, but you know that I only love you, my dearest Charlotte, and that if anyone could—"

He stopped mid-thought as Charlotte's mouth dropped open and her eyes went wide in alarm. Far too quickly, all color drained from his dear Charlotte's face.

"You are supposed to marry Lady Jenny?" Charlotte asked, her voice rising too fast.

Petrus winced, kicking himself for blurting things out like that without checking to see what Charlotte's understanding of the situation was first. He might have saved them both a bit of trouble, if he hadn't been so impetuous.

He sighed and took Charlotte's hand to lead her off to one side of the room, where they could sit by the crackling fire.

"As I understand it, my uncle, the king, does wish for me to marry Lady Jenny, yes," he confessed, deliberately sitting too close to Charlotte. Their knees touched, and he had yet to let go of her hand. "She was brought here shortly before I departed for England to investigate the Rathborne-Paxton family. But you must know that I have only ever felt friendship for Lady Jenny. I have never even considered marrying her, let alone loving her. My heart belongs to one woman and one woman alone."

He hoped Charlotte would find that a fanciful enough declaration to soothe her. Instead, Charlotte looked more distressed than ever.

"That is the matter, then," she said, staring at a spot on the carpet in front of them, caught up in her own thoughts. "Lady Jenny seems so forlorn because the man she was intended to marry has fallen in love with someone else."

She glanced up at him, as if appealing to Petrus to somehow make the situation right. Only, Petrus didn't think there was any possible way to make everyone happy. Not as things were.

"I know my uncle wants this, and that he believes strongly in family duty and loyalty," Petrus began. "But, my darling, you are the only—"

Again, Petrus was interrupted. This time by the sound of low voices and footsteps in the corridor, heading their way.

He didn't want to be caught alone with Charlotte. It would be bad for her reputation, and she was only just beginning to warm her way into the family. He needed to make Charlotte appear in the very best light so that when the time came to shatter his uncle's expectations and to go against the word of his king, he would be doing it to marry a woman his family loved and respected anyhow.

"Come," he whispered tightly, pulling Charlotte to stand, then whisking her around the back of the couch. "We can hide in here."

He tugged Charlotte over to a narrow door between two bookshelves. It led to a small closet lined with shelves, where the family kept games and puzzles and other things that entertained them through the long winter days. The closet smelled richly of cedar and pine. It was the perfect place to hide, not only because it was pleasant, but because it was narrow enough that he was forced to hold Charlotte pressed tightly against him so that they would fit.

He managed to shut the door just as Oskar and Uncle Milas strode into the room. He and Charlotte were able to observe everything happening in the library through the tiny holes in the pattern carved on the door.

"The family is everything, Oskar, you know that," Uncle Milas said, apparently frustrated with Oskar for some reason. "We have a duty to the people of this kingdom. You more than most."

Petrus wasn't certain what particular duty his uncle was talking about, but the admonishment hit Petrus hard. He had a duty to his family and his kingdom as well, whether he liked it or not.

"I understand, Father," Oskar said. "But marriage is one of the most powerful tools our kingdom has to secure its future peace and prosperity."

"Marriage is the cornerstone of family," Uncle Milas explained. Petrus could see his face through the lattice on the door, see how serious his uncle was. "Our subjects love us as they do not only because we have given them prosperity and freedom. They love us because we reflect the sort of love and family they would wish for themselves. We are a model for our subjects, and as such, it is only right, as you are of a certain age, to marry and continue with the family line."

"But marry who?" Oskar demanded. "I am not at liberty to make my own choices."

"Neither are you a slave to the crown," Uncle Milas argued. "Either way, you have an obligation to wed and be happy."

"How do I do that while advancing the interests of Aegiria? Do you propose I hold a ball and invite every princess in Europe just so I can make my own choice?"

"If necessary," Uncle Milas said with a shrug. "I would

not object to holding some sort of Cinderella ball, if you wished to emulate the fairy tale as a way to choose your beloved."

"I do not, Father," Oskar said with a deep scowl.

He might not have been happy about the prospect, but Petrus heard Charlotte's excited intake of breath near his ear and felt her body tighten as he held her. She thought that sort of ball was a grand idea.

"You know my feelings on this, Father," Oskar said, lowering his voice a bit. "You know why I cannot simply indulge my own fancies."

Something about the way his cousin spoke made Petrus frown. Something about it felt all too familiar.

Uncle Milas stepped closer to Oskar, clapping a hand on his shoulder. "You have a duty to your family, son," he said. "Think of how it would look if you had your own way in this?"

Cold prickles raced down Petrus's back. His uncle could have been speaking to him, for all the situation fit.

"Our people would be scandalized if they knew the truth of what you are proposing to do," Uncle Milas continued. "It would be a black mark against the family, against our honor and everything we stand for. Look at what is happening across Europe. Royal dynasties that have existed for hundreds of years have been falling throughout this century. Some of those monarchs have been killed by people who once loved them, all because their princes have not remained true to the principles of their kingdoms."

"The people of Aegiria are hardly likely to revolt because of who I marry, Father," Oskar said, but he didn't have the same intensity in his voice as he'd had before.

"Perhaps not," Uncle Milas said. "But we must do everything we can to keep our subjects happy. We are not in this position of privilege and power for ourselves. We exist for them. Therefore, I ask you to do this thing for me. You will find happiness, I swear it. We all will."

Oskar seemed to crumble a bit. He rubbed his forehead, then said, "Alright, Father. I will consider it."

Uncle Milas and Oskar exchanged a few more words as they headed out of the library. Petrus didn't hear them, though. He sagged against one side of the shelves, his heart beating in his throat, guilt pouring down on him.

"I think they're gone," Charlotte whispered, resting a hand on his chest over his heart. "Oh! My! Petrus, darling, your heart is pounding."

Petrus sighed and reached for the door handle. As much as he would have loved to stay hidden with Charlotte forever, he knew they couldn't live in their own little world forever.

He opened the door and stepped into the library, drawing Charlotte with him.

"Oh, dear," Charlotte said when she saw his expression. "That isn't an encouraging sight at all."

Charlotte took charge, leading Petrus back to the couch where they'd been seated before.

Once they were seated, she said, "It's what the king said about family duty and honor, isn't it."

Petrus sighed again. The conversation had been a bit cryptic, but he was certain he knew what Oskar and Uncle Milas had been speaking about. Neither he nor Oskar were at liberty to marry someone of their choosing.

He hated the way he would be forced to break Charlotte's heart, and his own for that matter. "I have a duty to my family, my king, and my kingdom," he said.

"To marry Lady Jenny," Charlotte said. Surprisingly, she spoke as though the situation were a puzzle that needed solving instead of the end of their beautiful, but far too short, acquaintance.

"I wish to marry you," he said, laying all of his cards on the table, even though it was not the most romantic way to almost propose.

Charlotte's face lit with joy, and she took both of Petrus's hands. "And I wish to marry you as well," she said, her voice bubbling with determination.

"I fear we might be kept from it, though, darling," he went on, his shoulders dropping. "Uncle Milas wants that alliance with Sweden, which means a political marriage. I am on the expendable side in this family, so I'm the one he's chosen to serve that purpose."

"Nonsense," Charlotte said, shaking her head with a practical look and scooting closer to him. "I do not believe that is what your uncle, a man who loves you, as I have seen with my own eyes, meant by his insistence on marrying the right woman."

"What else could he have meant?" Petrus asked with a shrug.

Charlotte didn't answer his question. She was too deep in thought. She shifted, facing the Christmas tree for a moment, as if it could give her focus.

"There has to be more to the situation that we are unaware of," she went on. "Or perhaps there is a way to dissuade Lady Jenny from hanging her heart on the hopes of marrying you. When I spoke to her earlier—"

"You spoke to her earlier?" Petrus was alarmed at the prospect.

"She seemed more concerned with leaving Aegiria than with losing you," Charlotte finished her thought. "I must believe *that* is her primary concern. There must be something back in Sweden that she wishes to avoid. If she stays here, she would have far more ability to determine her own life. Things in Aegiria are quite free for women. I have no wish to leave myself."

Her eyes turned soft with that final pronouncement, and

she smiled at Petrus as though neither of them had a care in the world.

"My uncle is the king," Petrus said, feeling far stupider than he wanted to for pointing out something so obvious. "Kings are to be obeyed."

"But even kings can have their minds changed," Charlotte said. "King Milas seems like a reasonable man. I am certain that if we work together, we can discover the truth of this situation and set everything to rights."

A rush of warmth filled Petrus, and he squeezed Charlotte's hand, which he still held, tighter. "I love you, Charlotte," he said, pouring more feeling into the words than he intended to. "I love you, and you give me strength. I know we can work our way through this maze." He slapped his free hand against his thigh and stood, taking her with him. "I will look for solutions in every corner and behind every Christmas decoration."

"That's the spirit," Charlotte said, beaming at him.

"You are right," he went on, feeling taller and stronger for her support. "There must be a solution to this problem. I can convince my uncle that the two of us are meant to be together and that all of Aegiria will be better for it."

"And I will help you in any way I can, my dearest," Charlotte said.

Petrus couldn't help himself. Charlotte was so wonderful and such a burst of sunlight that he swept her into his arms and kissed her again. Their bodies melded together as he held her and explored her mouth. It occurred to him that letting someone find them together like that could be a solution to everything, but he still had Charlotte's reputation to think about. Uncle Milas was just as likely to disapprove of Charlotte for allowing herself to be kissed out of wedlock, especially since Petrus was intended for someone else, as he was to decide he liked her.

"We must go about our business as usual," Petrus said, breathless as he ended their kiss. "A solution will present itself. We simply need to be looking out for it."

"Agreed," Charlotte said. "All will be well, I promise you."

Petrus loved her, but he wasn't certain that was a promise she could make.

Chapter Five

Christmas was only a few days away, and even though Charlotte did everything she could to endear herself to King Milas and Petrus's entire, extended family, she wasn't certain she was quite hitting the mark. Everyone treated her with absolute politeness, and she knew that they liked her well enough, but every time she might have had a chance to be seen at Petrus's side in a public situation, something or another, most frequently Crown Prince Oskar, kept them apart or pulled Petrus away.

Lady Jenny seemed to sense that her chances of winning Petrus and staying in Aegiria were slipping more and more as well. The poor woman was so quiet and so withdrawn, no matter what Charlotte tried to make her feel valued and included.

"This salmon dish is exquisite, and so unique," Charlotte commented to Lady Jenny across the table at supper, three days before Christmas. "And it is so pink. Do you enjoy the bright color, Lady Jenny?"

Lady Jenny seemed surprised that Charlotte was speaking to her at all. She seemed to have listed slightly at the table, where she was seated between Petrus and Prince Oskar again, dropping slightly toward Oskar's side. She straightened quickly, blinked rapidly, and said, "Yes." She then shook her head and drew her hand up from under the table to take her fork. "I believe the salmon is smoked rather than cooked, which is what gives it the pink color."

Charlotte smiled—it was encouraging that Lady Jenny had spoken to her at all—but sent Petrus a peek to see if there was anything that could be done.

"New potatoes with dill compliment the dish especially well," he said, then added, "Do you not think so, Lady Jenny?"

But Lady Jenny had drifted into her thoughts once more, and looked miserable because of it.

Which didn't make the slightest bit of sense to Charlotte, since Petrus had been the one to speak to her. It wasn't that Charlotte wanted Petrus to fawn over Lady Jenny or to turn her head, but if the two of them could at least become friends, then perhaps they could all get to the bottom of the situation.

"I hear we are to play another game this evening after supper," Charlotte tried again, only barely catching Lady Jenny's eyes to let her know it was she Charlotte was addressing. "Something called Huckle Buckle Beanstalk?"

"I am unfamiliar with the game," Lady Jenny said, then went back to her supper without looking at anyone.

Charlotte sent Petrus another look, along with a slight shrug, then continued to eat herself. She simply did not know what was wrong, and it was aggravating.

She wasn't the only one who noticed things were amiss.

"What is the matter with Lady Jenny?" Priya asked as the two of them took a small detour to the ladies' retiring room before joining the rest of the family in the library after supper. "She has been so sallow and withdrawn since we've arrived."

Charlotte finished washing her hands in the basin on one side of the room, biting her lip as she did. It wasn't her place to

49

share Lady Jenny's troubles, but Priya was like a sister to her, and she needed advice.

"There is a great deal more intrigue at the palace than any of us could have imagined," she said, turning to face Priya. "It turns out that Lady Jenny was brought here from Sweden specifically so that Petrus might marry her."

"Oh, dear." Priya pressed a hand to her chest. "Does that mean your beloved is already betrothed?"

Charlotte shook her head. "He is not. There is no understanding between them but that of family expectation."

"The family expects Petrus to marry Lady Jenny?" Priya blinked.

"King Milas would very much like him to, yes," Charlotte said. She frowned. "At least, that is what Petrus thinks." After the conversation between King Milas and Crown Prince Oskar she and Petrus had overheard the other day, she wasn't so certain. The king wanted Oskar to marry, that was true, but Lady Jenny's name was never brought up.

Priya thought for a moment, then focused her gaze on Charlotte. "You do not seem as upset as I would imagine."

"Because Petrus has made it quite clear that he loves me and wishes to marry me," Charlotte said, glad to announce that much to her dearest friend. She smiled as she did, but that smile dropped a bit too quickly. "Petrus feels torn between his obligation to his family—who have been so generous as to count him as one of their own, considering his manner of conception—and his love for me. We are attempting to seek a solution that will satisfy everyone."

Charlotte expected Priya to leap in and help her, but instead, her friend shook her head gravely. "I know a thing or two about family obligations where marriage is concerned," Priya said, taking Charlotte's arm and steering her out of the retiring room and down the hall toward the library. "Those sorts of obligations are difficult indeed to break or to get around."

"Difficult, yes, but not impossible," Charlotte insisted.

Priya glanced sideways at her. "You may have to prepare yourself for Petrus bowing to family pressures and marrying the woman his family has chosen for him."

Charlotte let out a small huff of annoyance. "I will not," she said. "Petrus is mine. Besides, something isn't right on Lady Jenny's end. I do not think she truly wishes to marry Petrus either. And yet, she confided in me that she does not want to return to Sweden. Only, her father has issued an ultimatum to her that if she is not engaged by Christmas, he will take her home by New Year's."

Priya frowned and hummed. "It is a muddle indeed," she said. They were right at the doorway to the library, so not much more could be said, but Priya turned to her and asked, "What are you planning to do to resolve the situation?"

"I do not know," Charlotte sighed. "You must help me keep watch for anything that might help."

"You know I will do anything to help you, dearest," Priya said with a smile.

The two of them entered the library arm in arm, ready to solve everything.

But the problem seemed too slippery for either of them to get a grasp on as the family gathered in the sitting area to one side of the Christmas tree so that Princess Elna, the oldest of the king and queen's daughters, could explain the rules of Huckle Buckle Beanstalk.

"This is the Huckle Buckle," Princess Elna said, holding up a small bit of ivory carved into the shape of an old Chinese man.

Charlotte and Priya took their places with the rest of the Rathborne-Paxton family, who listened closely to the instructions. Petrus moved subtly to stand by Charlotte's side. He looked at her with a question in his eyes, but Charlotte smiled at him to let him know all was well.

"Of course, any small object can be the Huckle Buckle," Princess Elna went on, "but this figurine has been in the family for generations, so we use this. If you play this game at home, you may use whatever object you like."

Charlotte nodded at the explanation, but her attention was on Lady Jenny, who stood between Prince Oskar and Princess Luna, her head downcast.

"To start with, I will hide the Huckle Buckle somewhere in the room," Princess Elna went on. "Somewhere in plain sight. Once I announce that the Huckle Buckle has been hidden, everyone will search for it. Without the use of hands, of course, since the object will be visible without having to remove anything. When you see it, shout out 'Huckle Buckle Beanstalk!', but do not retrieve the Huckle Buckle or point out to everyone where it is."

"The game works even better if you wait a few seconds before shouting so as to deflect from where you might have spotted the Huckle Buckle," Prince Lars said, a mischievous glint in his eyes.

Charlotte broke into a smile. She'd played games like that before, and yes, it was always more fun if one tried to pretend they'd seen the hidden object somewhere other than where they'd actually spotted it.

"I will start the hiding while the rest of you cover your eyes and count to twenty-five for the day of Christmas," Princess Elna said. "Are you ready?"

Everyone turned away or buried their faces in their hands or in the crooks of their arms. The entire assemblage began counting in unison.

As they did, Charlotte heard the shuffle of Princess Elna rushing away to hide the Huckle Buckle. Also, while everyone's eyes were closed and they were distracted with counting,

Charlotte felt Petrus's hand slide against the small of her back. She tried her best not to giggle or squirm as Petrus teased her by walking his fingers up her spine, but it was a nearly impossible feat.

"Twenty-three, twenty-four, twenty-five!"

They all finished counting in unison and opened their eyes. Immediately, everyone moved from where they were and began searching for the Huckle Buckle.

Charlotte was more interested in searching for a way to engage Lady Jenny in the fun so that she might figure out what the full picture of what had the poor woman in such distress. With a quick glance to Petrus, she tip-toed closer to Lady Jenny's side.

But before she could reach the woman to suggest that the two of them search together, Prince Oskar touched a hand to the small of Lady Jenny's back and gestured toward Petrus with his other arm.

"Perhaps you and Prince Petrus should search together, Lady Jenny," he suggested.

Charlotte's eyes widened in alarm, and she turned to Petrus to ask what she should do. Helping Lady Jenny was one thing, but it would help no one to encourage Lady Jenny all the way into Petrus's arms.

But it was already too late.

"I, er, yes," Lady Jenny said. She glanced toward Oskar with a dutiful but sad nod, then crossed the room to stand by Petrus. "I will search with you."

Charlotte frowned. "I didn't think the game was played in pairs," she muttered, a little surprised that those words ended up spoken aloud.

"We play however the rules tell us to play, Miss Sloane," Oskar said in a near whisper as he stepped past her, searching around the room. "We do not choose the rules."

He didn't sound happy about it. Not at all.

Charlotte wondered. Her attempts to search for the Huckle Buckle took her to one side of the room, which enabled her to glance back at the full scene and to take in the sight of Oskar searching, and Petrus looking around and trying to assist Lady Jenny as well. Oskar glanced back to Petrus and Lady Jenny. It couldn't possibly be that Oskar—

"Huckle Buckle Beanstalk!" Ellen shouted so loudly in her American accent that everyone in the room jumped. When they stared at her, Ellen shrugged and said, "That's the way it's meant to be done, right?"

"Huckle Buckle Beanstalk!" Mr. Samuel Rathborne-Paxton called out a moment later, but from an entirely different part of the room.

"Oh! Huckle Buckle Beanstalk!" the queen herself shouted a moment later.

Charlotte couldn't help but laugh. The pure delight that each of them expressed when they found the little ivory Chinese man was the perfect sort of festive accent to their gathering. It was enough to make her concentrate on the game so that she wouldn't be the last person to find the Huckle Buckle. Considering the royal family's penchant for making each other do embarrassing things as forfeits, there was no telling what would happen to the last person to locate the Huckle Buckle.

Fortunately, that person wasn't her. She spotted the Huckle Buckle peeking around the corner of a small clock on the mantelpiece shortly after Petrus called out Huckle Buckle Beanstalk on behalf of both himself and Lady Jenny. Priya ended up being the last one to find it, and her only forfeit was that she had to be the one to hide the Huckle Buckle next. Which wasn't much of a forfeit, to Charlotte's way of thinking.

The game continued for a few more rounds, and Charlotte found herself thinking that if not for the distraction of

Lady Jenny, she would have had a merry time indeed. Lady Jenny ended up being the first person to beg off and depart to go to bed, which relieved some of the tension. The entire party broke up soon after that, and everyone scattered and went their separate ways to bed.

"Miss Sloane, do you have a moment?" Petrus asked Charlotte as they reached the top of the stairs to the second floor, where the guest room Charlotte had been given was located.

"Certainly, your highness," Charlotte replied, playing along with the formality Petrus had shown her.

She crossed the landing at the top of the stairs to him. Petrus kept his back straight and glanced around as if he hadn't a care in the world, but Charlotte knew he was waiting until the hallway had emptied out.

Once they were mostly alone, but for a few servants moving around at the base of the stairs, Petrus grinned at her.

"You still have a forfeit to perform for me," he told her.

"I beg your pardon?" Charlotte said with mock shock, placing a hand on her chest.

Petrus laughed. "I caught you putting that wretched boot on the tree the other day fair and square, and I never demanded a forfeit from you."

"Whatever do you have in mind, sir?" Charlotte asked, feigning innocence.

"You'll have to come with me to find out," he said, a flash of mischief and desire in his eyes.

Charlotte had not fallen off the turnip cart yesterday. But she didn't protest Petrus's clear intentions. Neither did she run from them, when arguably she should have.

Instead, she grasped Petrus's hand with a breathless giggle and let him lead her on down the hallway and around a few corners to a different part of the palace.

"These are my private quarters," Petrus whispered after pulling her through a door into a lovely, quaint apartment.

The rooms appeared to be beautifully furnished and comfortable, and there was a stunning view of the harbor through the tall windows at one end of the room.

"My, my, Prince Petrus," Charlotte said, allowing herself to be drawn into his arms as soon as they were completely alone in the safety of the private apartment. "I fear my virtue is at risk at this moment."

Petrus laughed, then kissed her. It was so simple and so powerful. He didn't make speeches or attempt to coerce or seduce Charlotte. He simply kissed her with all the passion he felt—and she knew he felt it, because she felt it as well. They were in perfect accord as they twined their arms around each other and let their lips meet and explore each other's.

It was a beautiful, heated moment, and Charlotte knew it was a prelude to more, but she forced herself to pause, to rest her palms against Petrus's chest, and to stare up at him with a frank look.

"I very much approve of this forfeit," she said, facing the matter seriously, "but we must talk about Lady Jenny first."

Petrus sighed and slumped a bit. "There is only one woman I wish to think about tonight, and it is not Lady Jenny Lindstrom," he said.

"I know, darling," Charlotte said, playing with the buttons on his jacket. One of them popped open with her playing, so she decided to open the rest of them. "But we cannot think only of our own happiness without considering hers as well."

Petrus stilled Charlotte's hands and arched one eyebrow at her. "You aren't suggesting that I entertain the idea of marrying Lady Jenny, are you?"

"Not at all," Charlotte said. "But I like the woman and I do wish there was something we could do for her. She wants to stay in Aegiria."

"Then we shall find a way for her to stay," Petrus said, his body moving against hers in a way that left Charlotte breathless. "We shall find a way for you to stay as well, my darling."

He kissed her again, wrapping his arms around her and holding her possessively. His mouth was commanding as it slanted over hers in another kiss. Whether it was the boldness of being alone in a place where they absolutely would not be disturbed or the excitement of the evening giving Petrus courage, Charlotte didn't care. She was more than ready to be thoroughly debauched, no matter what it might mean for her reputation. It banished all thoughts about Lady Jenny, and her questions about Prince Oskar, from her mind.

And honestly, she felt as though succumbing to Petrus's charms wasn't much of a gamble at all. She trusted Petrus, trusted him with her life and her person. She trusted him to draw her across the apartment to his bedroom, and to help her undo all the fiddly fastenings of her gown. She even trusted him when he removed his own clothing piece by piece, revealing a powerful and somewhat intimidating physique under them.

"You don't have to look if the sight is too much," Petrus said just as he unbuttoned his drawers and prepared to remove them.

Charlotte had already finished removing her clothing and was just sliding between the cool, crisp sheets of Petrus's bed. "Oh, no," she said, twisting to her side and making herself comfortable as she watched him. "This is a sight I wouldn't miss for all the world."

Petrus's brow flew up, and he failed to stifle a laugh. "Have I fallen in love with a minx, then?" he asked.

"You'll never know until you drop those drawers and join me," she said, hoping her look was as tempting as the sight before her.

Petrus laughed outright and quickly divested himself of his drawers. Charlotte had only the briefest sight of his bare thighs and the thick spear of his manhood—which made her gasp and salivate—before he hurried into the bed with her.

She didn't need to see his naked body in all its glory then. She could feel it, and there was so much to feel. Petrus rolled her to her back straight away and settled himself between her thighs, prompting her to spread them wider, as he bent to kiss her. The beautiful sensation of his mouth on hers and his tongue teasing hers was eclipsed by the lean, heavy lines of his body as he pressed down on her.

He managed to cover her in such a way that wasn't too much of a burden. The way he supported himself with his hands on either side of her as he kissed her and lowered himself until the hair on his chest tickled her breasts was a revelation of the highest order. Charlotte knew it made her wanton and wicked, but she circled her arms and legs around him anyhow, utterly not caring.

"I've wanted this nearly from the first moment we met," she sighed as Petrus moved from ravishing her mouth to kissing and nibbling his way down her neck to her shoulder.

"You have?" Petrus asked, pausing to lift above her again so he could gaze down at her in the flickering light of the lantern he'd lit when they'd entered the room.

Charlotte laughed impishly. "Does it shock you to know that your sweet beloved is not quite the fainting violet that women are supposed to be?"

"You aren't?" This time, Charlotte couldn't quite tell if Petrus's shock was feigned or if he really was upset by her forwardness.

"That is, I mean, I have never lain with a man before," she rushed to say. "Only that I am not ignorant of relations, and I have dearly hoped that you might be the man to demonstrate in actuality all the things I have come to know in theory."

Petrus both surprised and relieved her by laughing. His body softened a bit as he dipped down to kiss her again. "That might be the strangest and most endearing way anyone has ever tried to seduce me in my life."

Charlotte wanted to come up with a reply to that, but all words were blasted from her as Petrus stroked one hand along her side, bringing it up to play with her breast. He kissed his way down her neck and shoulder again, continuing until his lips met his hand around her breast. The sensation was blissful, and she gave herself over to it, arching into Petrus's touch and his kisses.

Part of Charlotte felt she should participate more fully as Petrus all but worshiped her body. He knew precisely how to kiss and stroke her to leave her shivering and breathless. Any fear or hesitance she might have had to give herself over so fully that way melted with the press of Petrus's lips against her belly, her hip, and the inside of her thigh.

Time after time, she attempted to push herself to tell Petrus how much she enjoyed his touch and how deeply she trusted him to do what was right for her, and time after time, the words changed into sighs and moans of pleasure as he fed something within her that Charlotte had only dreamed to think of.

She should have been shocked when he brought his mouth to that private place between her legs, but she only writhed and moaned and opened her legs wider for him to do whatever he wanted with her down there. The things he was able to do with his fingers and his tongue had her body coiling tight and pulsing with need.

When he closed his mouth around a particular part of her and began to lick and suck with perfect strokes, Charlotte burst apart, crying out as her body throbbed with pleasure. She'd been able to produce a similar effect for herself in the past, but having Petrus wring that pleasure from her was a thousand times better in every way.

He didn't hesitate—and she was glad he didn't—in sliding

his way up her body and bringing his staff right to her entrance. She was still caught up in the pleasure of it all when he pushed firmly inside her. The invasion brought with it a brief moment of shock and the feeling that something had torn, but thankfully her mother had warned her of such things. She allowed the sensation to pass without too much worry, canceling out any anxiety the moment might have caused by wrapping her arms and legs around Petrus again as he thrust into her.

It was so much better than she'd been led to believe it was. Her pleasure had subsided a bit, but continued to simmer as she held Petrus fast and let his desire build and build to the point where he moved and grunted and thrust into her as nature intended. It was exciting and humbling to hold so much power in her arms, and when his pleasure reached its peak and burst with a few final thrusts and groans of satisfaction, Charlotte smiled.

She'd done that. She had turned this magnificent prince into a wild thing that needed her. She had submitted to him, but he had given himself over to her with just as much completeness. It was the way lovers were meant to be together, the way two souls that belonged together were meant to join.

"I love you, Petrus," Charlotte panted as Petrus pulled out of her and slumped to her side. She turned so that she could wriggle against him, even though they were both too hot for such cuddling. "I love you dearly, and I will do whatever needs must be done for the two of us to be together."

There had to be a way. Family obligations and Lady Jenny Lindstrom's feeling aside, there simply had to be a way for her and Petrus to be together.

Chapter Six

Petrus had not been some sort of saint in his life thus far, but neither had he been a complete rake, like his natural father, nor one to seduce women willy-nilly. Waking up with Charlotte in his bed, tucked against him and breathing softly in sleep, and remembering what they'd shared the night before was a singular and beautiful experience.

It must have been the high spirits of the game they'd all played and the general merriment of Christmas that had inspired him to take that extra step and to invite Charlotte into his bed. He'd been half in jest when he'd begun things the night before and had been surprised and delighted when Charlotte had come to him with no resistance. A part of him thought he should have been scandalized by a woman who would allow herself to be ruined so easily, but that part grumbled to him in Oskar's stuffy voice, and Petrus didn't feel as though anything about Charlotte had been ruined.

Charlotte was his and he was hers. They'd already spoken of marriage, and as soon as the moment presented itself, he would speak to his mother to secure her blessing and make the match formal.

Of course, he would have to gain Uncle Milas's approval as well, but even the king wouldn't deny true love.

Charlotte shifted beside Petrus, stretching as she woke up. Her movements against his body were sweet and tempting, and he had to draw in a breath and steel himself to keep from rolling her to her back and making love to her again. Once was beautiful, special, and memorable, but the more they indulged, the greater the risk that they would be forced to marry under less than respectable circumstances.

"Good morning, my darling," Petrus greeted her as Charlotte blinked her still-sleepy eyes open.

Charlotte mumbled as if she wasn't fully awake yet and snuggled closer to him with a yawn. She wriggled until she was half spread over him, then rested her head on his chest and closed her eyes again.

Petrus smiled, warmed from the inside out. His beloved was the most wonderful and fascinating creature God had ever made. It could be argued she was thoroughly unsuitable to be a prince's bride, but his natural brothers had all married unsuitable women, so why not him as well?

He'd made up his mind to let Charlotte slumber on, using his chest as a pillow, when Charlotte gasped and sat up so suddenly Petrus flinched.

"I'm here," Charlotte said on a sharp exhale, glancing fitfully around the room. "I'm here, with you."

Petrus was tempted to laugh at the degree of her alarm, but instead he said, "Yes you are, my dear. You're right where you belong."

He sat up as well, pulling her into his arms and stroking her back to try to soothe her. He even kissed her shoulders and would have lavished attention on her magnificent breasts, which he could now see in the light of day, but he wanted the moment to be about the connection between them, not about lust.

Charlotte softened for a moment, leaning into him and raising a hand to stroke his stubbly cheek. "You are handsome in the morning, all in a state of dishabille like this," she said with a smile, then touched her lips to his in a feather-light kiss that went straight to Petrus's heart.

He started to tighten his arms around her and rethink his determination not to make love to her again when Charlotte sucked in another breath and pulled away from him.

"What is the time?" she asked, wriggling for the end of the bed. "I should be back in my own bedchamber. I would hate to cause trouble by being found with you in such a state so early in the morning. Ooh, it's cold!"

The last bit came out louder and sharper than the rest of her words and was accompanied by Charlotte dancing from foot to foot and hugging herself so she could rub her arms as she searched for her clothing from the night before.

There was something so artless and adorable about her unguarded ways that Petrus could only smile. He loved how unpretentious Charlotte was. She was so unlike Lady Jenny, and although Petrus did admire the Swedish noblewoman, he would have chosen Charlotte over her a thousand times over, even with her humble birth.

"Never fear," he said, climbing out of bed to help her gather her clothing and dress, strangely unbothered by his own nakedness. "I will make certain you are returned to your own room before anyone in the palace sees you."

Although, he knew it might be a challenge to whisk her past some of the servants, who would be up early, lighting fires to ward off the chill of the frosty morning.

"Thank you," Charlotte told him with genuine gratitude. "You are a prince among men." She paused in the middle of donning her corset, then laughed. "Well, I suppose you truly *are* a prince, among men or otherwise."

The two of them laughed together, then hurried through

the arduous process of dressing to the point that they would not cause a scandal simply by being seen in the hallways undressed. As Charlotte finished with her fiddly buttons, Petrus dressed in the simplest pair of trousers and shirt he owned, throwing a dressing gown over it all. He could just barely get away with wearing a dressing gown in the halls of the palace, as long as they stayed in the private hallways.

Once they were marginally presentable, Petrus took Charlotte's hand and led her through his apartment to the hallway running through the entire wing of the palace. He opened the door carefully and peeked into the hall before allowing Charlotte to be revealed at all, and when he was satisfied the hall was abandoned, he gestured for Charlotte to follow him.

The hallways of the palace were quite dim in the mornings, but they weren't dark. Several lanterns in wall sconces were turned down low, providing enough light for the servants who lit the fires to make their way through the vast building without bumping into things. It was enough light to show Petrus the way down the hall to the juncture at the top of the stairs that divided the family quarters from the guest suites.

The tricky part was dashing across that exposed section of hall that opened out to the high ceilings of the grand staircase and the foyer below. Petrus motioned for Charlotte to wait just inside the hallway leading to the family apartments as he stepped out to take a look. But a door shut somewhere behind them, prompting Charlotte to squeal in giddy fright and to leap out into the juncture with him.

"Someone is coming," she whispered, unable to keep her laughter inside.

That set Petrus to laughing as well as he grabbed Charlotte's hand and dashed across to the guest hall with her.

It was impossible to maintain any sense of decorum from there. They both giggled up a storm as they hurried down the guest hallway, like two children caught searching for gifts from

Santa Claus in their parents' cupboards. Charlotte made him feel young again, like life was filled with joy and possibility. It was one of the many things he loved about her.

With a feeling of both relief and sadness, they reached the door to Charlotte's guest room.

"That was wonderful," she whispered as she grabbed hold of the doorhandle. Petrus could tell from the spark in her eyes that she meant their dash through the halls and everything they'd done the night before. "I most definitely think we should do it again," she continued, lowering her head a bit and making eyes at him.

Petrus's heart danced against his ribs, and his cock twitched as if it wanted to get started on their next time immediately. He pulled Charlotte away from the door and into his arms so that he could kiss her as lingeringly as he dared.

"We will most definitely do it all again," he whispered to her. "And I shall speak to all the people who need to be spoken to so that we might do it every night for the rest of our lives."

Charlotte giggled, her eyes sparkling with loving mischief. "See that you do," she told him with mock scolding, then pried herself away from him and dashed into her room.

As soon as she shut the door, Petrus leaned against the wall, smiling to himself with his eyes closed, and just feeling the adoration he had for Charlotte. The two of them would be so happy together, always entertaining each other, and building a life that would be the envy of all. He pushed away from the wall and headed swiftly back to the family wing, already thinking up arguments he could use to convince his uncle that he should be allowed to marry Charlotte, and that Lady Jenny would be taken care of one way or another.

Those thoughts were cut abruptly short as he turned the corner into the connecting hallway only to nearly run headlong into Lady Jenny herself. The woman was hurrying as though the Hound of Asgard were chasing her. She was dressed in a nightgown and dressing gown with her hair in disarray down her back, and when she thumped into Petrus, she yelped and started to shake.

"Lady Jenny," Petrus said, steadying her, then deliberately stepping away so as not to overwhelm her. "Are you quite well? Is something the matter?"

Petrus had already started making a list of all the things that might have startled Lady Jenny enough to have her out of bed so early in the morning, but those thoughts took on another shade of meaning when she glanced back to the family wing of the house, as if she'd come from there and not up the stairs from the public part of the palace.

"I...I...that is...I was just...." The poor woman turned bright red and began fiddling with the sleeves of her robe. After her one look back to the family wing, she seemed to deliberately not look in that direction. "I couldn't...."

Petrus couldn't allow the poor woman to continue to flail. "It is alright, Lady Jenny. As you see, I am up and about for my own reasons this morning as well."

"Yes," Lady Jenny said. She lowered her head and looked as though she might burst into tears.

Petrus couldn't let that pass either.

"My lady, are you certain all is well with you?" he asked what he perhaps should have asked long before. "Only, you've seemed so distressed of late, and I would hate to think that I had a hand in that."

His suspicions about Lady Jenny's reasons for being upset seemed to be confirmed as she glanced woefully up at him. "It is not your fault, your highness," she said in a tiny, hopeless voice. "It is just...I am stuck...you see...."

Petrus did not see, and when Lady Jenny lowered her head and let out a plaintive sob, it tugged hard on Petrus's heart-strings.

"Please tell me all," he said, inching closer to her, but

without any real desire to touch her. "Perhaps the problem can be solved."

"It cannot," Lady Jenny sobbed, glancing up at him with glassy eyes. "For, you see, my father sent me here for a specific purpose."

Petrus swallowed hard. He knew full well what that purpose was, and his part in it.

Lady Jenny seemed to know that he knew. The two of them stared at each other for a long moment before she continued with, "I have failed at that purpose, and *Far* has said he will call me home before the new year if I am not engaged by Christmas."

Petrus winced. He'd suspected something like that, but had deliberately avoided thinking about it because of the position it placed him—and Charlotte—in.

"I take it you do not wish to return to Sweden?" he asked quietly.

Lady Jenny started to look over her shoulder toward the family wing, but stopped herself at the last minute and shook her head. "I do not," she said in a squeak. "I...I love...." She bit her lip and fretted with the hems of her sleeves. "I love Aegiria so, and I wish to live my life here."

Petrus wondered if that was what she'd started out saying. He wondered if Lady Jenny had been about to confess something to him that would hurt for him to hear. She had come to Aegiria to be his bride, after all, and things like that could ignite in a woman's imagination. He could not recall doing anything specifically to make the poor woman fall in love with him, but the promise of being a princess and living a fairy tale life could have made a home in her imagination.

And if Lady Jenny had somehow convinced herself she was in love with him, if her heart would be broken by being sent back to Sweden, he felt deeply responsible for that. The guilt of it was almost too much, particularly as he could never love Lady Jenny. He was Charlotte's and she was his.

"Never fear, my lady," he told Lady Jenny anyhow. "We will come up with something. I promise you that."

The grateful way Lady Jenny looked up at him, with tears clumping her lashes, shot straight to Petrus's heart—in a platonic way, a way that made him feel responsible.

"Go back to your room now and prepare to face the day," he told her. "I will think on this matter and determine what can be done."

Lady Jenny nodded, and without saying another word, she hurried on into the guest wing.

Petrus frowned and rubbed a hand over the lower half of his face. He started on to the family wing slowly, rolling the problem around and around in his head. His whole heart was with Charlotte, but his duty to his family could not be discounted so lightly. He owed so much to his family. If it came down to it, if the king ordered him to go through with his intentions for him and Lady Jenny, he wasn't certain he would be at liberty to disobey.

Those thoughts were still rolling restlessly in his mind when he entered the family wing and spotted Brigitta coming out of her apartment. Of course, his intrepid sister was already dressed for the day and looking as though she were ready to take on an invading army, like some sort of Viking princess, like their mother.

Brigitta took one look at Petrus and burst into a snorting laugh. "Well, well. What have we here? Wandering the halls of the palace in your nightclothes, are you?"

Normally, Petrus would have joined in with her joking, but his heart was too troubled.

"I've just encountered Lady Jenny in the corridor," he said, gesturing back toward the staircase so that Brigitta would not get the wrong idea. "She's told me something quite disturbing."

Brigitta lost her teasing demeanor and strode down the hall to meet him.

"What is it?" she asked. "Is something wrong? Is she ill?"

Petrus vaguely knew that Brigitta and Lady Jenny had become close friends, but he hadn't realized how deep that friendship was until he saw the concern in his sister's eyes.

That only added another layer to his pressing sense of responsibility.

"Did you know that her father has said if she isn't engaged to me by Christmas, he'll take her home before the new year?" he asked.

Brigitta's eyes went wide, and she grabbed Petrus's arm. "She's intimated as much to me before, as well as lamenting over how hopeless the situation feels to her, but she hasn't yet come out and said it in so many words."

Petrus let out a heavy breath. "I don't know what to do, Brig. I...I cannot marry Lady Jenny."

"Because you are practically engaged to Miss Sloane already," Brigitta said.

Petrus's brow shot up. "How do you know that?"

Brigitta laughed and shook her head. "Men are so very thick when it comes to recognizing matters of the heart, especially when those things are right in front of them."

Petrus felt his face heat. "Have Charlotte and I been that obvious?"

"Yes, you have," Brigitta said, her teasing look returned.

"Which must be why Lady Jenny is so distressed," Petrus said, his shoulders dropping. "She knows her chances of having me are almost nil now." He glanced directly at his sister. "But what am I to do? It pains me to think I am ruining a woman's life by not loving her." Especially when, not half an hour before, he had been worried about ruining Charlotte by loving her too much.

"Uncle Milas wants you to marry Lady Jenny," Brigitta said, expressing the other part of the problem. "He wants the diplomatic alliance with Sweden. And Lord Lindstrom not only has influence with King Oscar of Sweden, he has made himself a powerful industrial fortune. Uncle Milas is desperate for the connection."

Petrus sighed and sank to lean against the wall, scrubbing his hands through his hair.

"What am I to do, Brig?" he appealed to his sister. "I love Charlotte more than anything, but I have a duty to our family. And Lady Jenny is a good and kind woman."

"That is no reason to marry her when you love someone else," Brigitta said. "Even if our uncle wants it."

"But is my happiness worth losing an important diplomatic connection for the family and the kingdom?" Petrus asked, genuinely not knowing the answer. "I have a duty to my family, my king, and my kingdom. Is love more powerful than that?"

"I want to say yes," Brigitta said, slouching against the wall opposite Petrus.

Petrus raised one eyebrow. "You want to, but you cannot?"

Brigitta chewed her lip and glanced across at him. "You still have two days before Christmas. That's two days to figure out a way to make Uncle Milas happy, Lady Jenny's father happy, and yourself happy."

"If it were my happiness alone at stake, I would propose to Charlotte directly," Petrus said.

"And that is the trouble with being a royal," Brigitta sighed. "As plain and logical as things may seem to the rest of the world, those same rules do not apply to us. We are not always at liberty to give our hearts away where we choose."

The thought made Petrus wince, partially because he hated it when Brigitta sounded like Oskar. He also stared hard at his sister and asked, "If Uncle Milas decided on a man you should marry, would you agree to the match, regardless of your feelings about the groom?"

Brigitta winced. "I suppose I would have to," she said. "Though it would greatly depend on who that groom of choice was."

Petrus nodded, then pushed away from the wall. He moved to rest a hand on Brigitta's arm and to kiss her forehead.

"All we can do at this point is wait and see what happens," he said. "While also keeping an eye out for any sort of magical solution that might present itself."

"I hope for your sake a solution does appear," Brigitta said. "I like Miss Sloane, and I can see how happy she makes you."

"She makes me blissfully happy," Petrus agreed with a smile.

But he knew full well exactly what they'd just been talking about. Just because a course of action might make a royal happy, that didn't mean they were at liberty to pursue it.

Chapter Seven

C harlotte had never been one to rest on the laurels of her own happiness when she knew that others were still in distress. As joyful as she felt after her illicit evening with Petrus, and as confident as she was that Petrus would formally propose to her before her visit to Aegiria was over, she knew she could never be truly happy while the threat of being taken away from Aegiria still hung over Lady Jenny.

"It isn't that I wish for Petrus to marry the poor woman to save her," she confided in Priya and the other Rathborne-Paxton brides as the five of them sat around a table in the center of the ballroom, hastily crafting more bows that would adorn the palace for the Christmas Eve ball on the morrow. "Petrus and I have an understanding, and I do not believe he would ever go back on that."

Nanette eyed Charlotte warily as she fastened a bow together with thin wire on the other side of the table. "Do you truly think that?" she asked. "Not to say that he doesn't love you and wish to marry you," she rushed on. "But I've performed in enough dramas where one or the other lover was forced to marry someone else for the sake of family duty."

"But this isn't a play," Ellen argued, using the spool of ribbon she'd just picked up to emphasize her point. "This is real life. In my experience, real life is far less dramatic than what is seen on a stage."

Alice laughed outright at this, though not unkindly. "This from a woman who comes from the Wild West of America." She turned to Charlotte and said, "Did you have a chance to attend that Wild West show in Earl's Court when they performed there a few years back?"

Charlotte could feel herself on the verge of an entire other conversation that she would very much liked to have had with Alice, but Priya interrupted by saying, "Family obligation is not something to be taken lightly." She looked at Charlotte with deepest concern. "I would hate to see you hurt from raising your hopes too high where Prince Petrus is concerned."

Of course Priya would be the wet blanket of the bunch. That didn't stop Charlotte from loving her cautious friend, though.

"I have ample reason to believe that Petrus would not cast me off at this point," she said, eyes downcast, face heating. "Particularly not after the other night."

She peeked up to find the Rathborne-Paxton brides all staring at her with varying degrees of surprise and amusement.

"Well done," Alice said at last with a hearty laugh.

"Well done indeed," Nanette grinned along with her. She straightened a bit, then added, "Though men have been known to wriggle out of promises for much less than that."

Charlotte shook her head and stood to begin gathering finished bows from the table and place them in a basket. "Petrus would never do that. I am confident in his love."

She smiled to herself as she spoke and plucked bows from the table to add to the basket with a spring in her step.

That spring flattened a bit as she spotted King Milas approaching the other end of the ballroom, where Petrus,

Prince Oskar, and several of Petrus's cousins were working to hang decorations around the top of the wall, using ladders and hammers. The king called up to Petrus, who scrambled down from the ladder to speak to him.

Charlotte held her breath, wishing she was close enough to that end of the room to hear what the king had to say. He seemed serious, whatever it was, and even across the distance, it was plain that his words had shifted Petrus's mood from jolly to sober. Oskar looked equally somber, perhaps even more so.

Charlotte hadn't realized she was standing still watching the men until Petrus glanced in her direction. The intensity of his stare felt like he'd fired an arrow into her heart. She even gulped for breath and stood straighter. She tried with everything she had to send her beloved a look of encouragement, but when King Milas and Oskar turned to glance in her direction, the arrows fired at her seemed to sting.

"Oh, dear," Ellen said, as though she'd been privy to everything the three men had said. "That doesn't seem good at all."

It might have been even worse than that, because Charlotte realized that she was not the only lady that the three men were staring at. Lady Jenny had just entered the ballroom as well. She carried long ropes of some sort of golden decoration in her arms, and Charlotte had to admit that the effect of so much gold surrounding the beautiful woman was as if an angel had descended into the room.

The terrible thought hit her right then. She would never be as beautiful and refined as Lady Jenny Lindstrom. She had not been born into nobility, like Lady Jenny. When she glanced back to the three men and found King Milas smiling at Lady Jenny with approval, her heart sank even further. It was obvious that, if given a chance between his nephew marrying a Swedish noblewoman of impeccable pedigree or the daughter of a British industrialist who hadn't quite lost the rough edges of his birth, Charlotte would not be his first choice.

"Prince Petrus doesn't look at Lady Jenny the way he looks at you," Alice said, breaking Charlotte out of the downward spiral of her thoughts. She turned to Alice, who went on with, "Anyone with eyes can see that, even a king."

Charlotte sighed and continued around the table, adding finished bows to the basket. "I suppose you're right. I only wish that the king would look beyond the interests of his kingdom to understand the hearts of his family members."

As soon as the words were out of her mouth, Charlotte realized how silly they sounded. Kings were responsible to their kingdoms above all. King Milas might like her as much as Lady Jenny, but he would press for his kinsmen to do what was right for Aegiria.

The three men said their final words to each other and went their separate ways. King Milas exited the ballroom, and after hesitating for a moment, Prince Oskar followed him. Petrus sent Charlotte an encouraging smile that didn't quite seem complete, then scurried back up the ladder that his brother stepped in to hold to continue with hanging decorations.

Charlotte finished gathering the completed ribbons, then headed to the windows, where Queen Sylvia was directing the entire operation. Charlotte was mightily impressed with the royal family's tradition of doing what servants would normally do and decorating the palace themselves. It made all the princes and princesses seem so much more human, in a way.

But with humanity came human frailty and the possibility of making mistakes. And as Charlotte reached the queen, so did Lady Jenny.

"You wanted these, your majesty," Lady Jenny said, presenting her armful of golden garlands.

"Yes, dear," the queen said, smiling affectionately at Lady Jenny. "You were so good to fetch them for me."

Charlotte swallowed. It was just a simple compliment, but did it mean that the queen liked Lady Jenny more than her?

She shook the thought away as unhelpful. It was a good thing that Lady Jenny was liked. Charlotte had a feeling the woman needed that sort of support. It was only a shame that that support seemed to come at Charlotte's own expense.

"We will hang the garlands from the windows," the queen directed Lady Jenny. "They will sparkle beautifully in the candlelight." She glanced to Charlotte with some warmth, but perhaps not quite as much? "And how can I help you, Miss Sloane?" she asked.

A sudden wave of anxiety swept over Charlotte. What if the queen and king didn't approve of her? What if they refused to allow Petrus to marry her, whether Lady Jenny was a consideration or not?

Charlotte forced herself to smile and ignore her worries in favor of what was right in front of her. Worrying about tomorrow had never accomplished anything.

"Where would you like these bows hung, your majesty?" she asked with what she hoped was kindness and amiability.

The queen smiled at her in a way that put Charlotte at ease. At least, for a moment.

"I think those can be hung in the parlors where refreshments will be served," the queen said. "Could you take them there directly? I believe Marta is in charge of decorating those rooms."

Marta was the palace housekeeper. The refreshment parlors were at the other end of the palace. The queen had more or less just sent her on an errand that would take her far away from the ballroom and from Petrus while simultaneously commanding Lady Jenny to engage in an activity that could throw her and Petrus together.

Charlotte did her very best not to put too much interpretation on things. "Yes, your majesty," she said, curtsying slightly, then turning to take the bows where they were needed.

As soon as she left the ballroom, her cheery smile dropped into a frown. She should not let her imagination run away with her. The queen's instructions were simply that, instructions to help with a long-held family tradition to prepare for a ball that would entertain everyone in the city on the morrow. She was not being sent away or snubbed or otherwise told she was inferior.

It was just that she adored Petrus and wanted to marry him so desperately that the fear of something swooping in and ruining that was strong.

Those thoughts were still burning within her as she cut across the hallway where most of the family's private rooms were located, only to run into Prince Oskar marching in the other direction. She wouldn't have given the dour expression on the prince's face much thought or done more than nod to him, but of all things, the prince appeared to have been crying.

But no, that was impossible. Oskar was the crown prince, the heir to the throne. He was a strong and stalwart man, and he had nothing to cry about.

"Your royal highness, is everything alright?" Charlotte paused to ask as they crossed paths.

Prince Oskar froze as though Charlotte had thrown ice water on him. He turned to blink at her.

"Nothing is wrong," he said, though his voice was tight. "Why would you assume anything was wrong?"

"I am sorry, your royal highness," Charlotte said with a slight curtsy. "It is just that you seem a bit upset."

Charlotte bit her lip, wondering how much she dared to confront a future king. Because Oskar didn't move to run away or dismiss her, she took a step closer to him.

"I know I am only an Englishwoman and far beneath the entire royal family, but I do care about your happiness and the happiness of your entire family," she said softly, managing a nice smile for him. "I've noticed that you've been slightly off of late, and I do apologize if I've had anything to do with that." She swallowed quickly, then added, "I apologize if my... friendship with your cousin has caused a disturbance in the course of the royal family's plans."

Oskar stared hard at her, then blinked. All at once, he let out his breath, and his entire countenance changed.

"It is not that, Miss Sloane," he said, managing a weak smile for her. "Your presence is not what has caused the trouble. No, indeed, I have found you to be sweet and charming, and I know my cousin adores you." He paused briefly, then sighed and rubbed his forehead. "That is the problem."

Charlotte frowned, not entirely certain what he meant by that. "Is there anything I can do?" she asked.

Oskar dropped his hands and shrugged. The gesture made him look much younger than he was. "I do not know," he said, then suddenly looked as if he might weep. "I simply do not know."

With that, he turned and marched off in a hurry.

Charlotte stared at his retreating back, even more flummoxed than she'd been before. She tried to make sense of the conversation, but none of the pieces fit. Granted, she had theories, but the evidence, so far, wasn't supporting them. So she continued on, searching out the parlor where Marta was waiting for the bows.

Her path took her directly past the library, and as she glanced into the room, not thinking much of it, she froze at the sight of King Milas hanging the hideous boot ornament on the tree.

It was a moment she couldn't resist.

"I've caught you!" she announced as she rushed into the room. "I've caught you in the act!"

King Milas started so violently that he nearly dropped the ornament. He fumbled it, his eyes wide, before hanging it on a bough. Then he faced Charlotte for a moment, his mouth working as though he would come up with some excuse for being where he was.

The moment was enough to make Charlotte laugh despite herself. A king was fidgeting before her as if he were a boy who had been caught stealing pies.

At last, the king blew out a breath, and his body sagged. "You have, indeed, caught me, Miss Sloane." He even laughed a bit and rubbed his forehead with the admission.

Charlotte's heart raced as she walked closer to him. She could find a way to use the situation, to use the forfeit she was due, to resolve the situation they were all in. But it would in no way be as simple as telling the king he must allow Petrus to marry her as his forfeit. That would result in Lady Jenny's banishment. She couldn't demand that the king keep Lady Jenny in Aegiria either. That was not his decision, that was Lord Lindstrom's.

But perhaps there was a way to start the gears turning in the machine that would resolve everything.

"I am at your service, Miss Sloane," the king said with a regal bow. "What forfeit would you have of me."

An idea blinked into Charlotte's mind. "I would like you to tell me a story, your majesty," she said, walking to one of the room's couches. She sat, putting the basket of bows on the floor beside her, then patted the other side of the couch as an indication the king should join her.

King Milas blinked in surprise, but also smiled. "What story would you like me to tell?" he asked, moving to sit with Charlotte, keeping his back straight and his mien majestic the whole time. "I'd wager you haven't heard some of the finer folk tales of Aegiria," he suggested.

"I should love to hear those, your majesty," Charlotte said with a smile designed to charm. "But it is another story I wish to hear from you right now."

The king looked intrigued. Better than that, he looked as though he liked Charlotte and admired her pluck. "What story is that, my dear?" he asked in a paternal voice.

Charlotte smiled. "I should like to hear the story of how you and Queen Sylvia met and fell in love."

For a moment, the king looked startled. Then something came over him that made him practically glow from the inside.

"That is my very favorite story to tell," he said, pink coming to his cheeks and light to his blue eyes.

"Go on," Charlotte said, matching his enthusiasm and scooting closer to him.

"We were so young," King Milas began, shaking his head and chuckling. "I was as full of myself as Oskar is now. I'd been sent abroad, to Copenhagen, for my education. I chose Copenhagen over Stockholm or London or Paris, because my family had once gone on holiday by the shores of Lake Furesø. I remembered seeing a blonde nymph bathing in the water every morning when I went out for my daily walk. Something told me that if I went back to Copenhagen, I might see that nymph again."

"And did you?" Charlotte asked, beaming as she guessed where the story was headed.

"I did," King Milas said. "It was more than a month after I'd arrived and taken up my student lodgings. I'd been invited to a ball at a country house just outside of the city. I attended with several of my mates, and, being a foolish and raucous student with too much time and money, my only intention was to eat and drink too much and to carouse.

"But there she was," he continued, his eyes unfocused and

dreamy. "The crowd of dancers parted, and I saw my Sylvia standing there in a gown of the same blue as the waters of Lake Furesø. I knew at once she was my nymph. I approached her directly and asked her to dance. We danced the entire night away, simply enjoying each other's company."

"And then you told the story of the nymph and she confessed it was her?" Charlotte asked, her heart beating wildly.

King Milas laughed aloud. "I told her the story, and she said that she had never been to Lake Furesø in her life."

Charlotte laughed along with him at the twist in the story.

"She thought it was romantic of me to pick her out for that reason," the king went on. "We had a good laugh over it. That laughter led to much more, and by Christmas of that year, I asked her to marry me and be my queen."

The king continued to smile fondly at the memory, and Charlotte's heart beat even faster. She could feel the moment to say something upon her.

"It is a wonderful thing when two young people in love find each other and know that they are meant for each other," she said, lowering her head a bit and glancing up at him through her lashes.

King Milas came out of his thoughts and grinned at her knowingly. "I am not the one standing in the way of true love, Miss Sloane," he said frankly, with just a hint of mystery. "I am too old and too well-versed in the ways of the world to prevent people who should be together from marrying."

Charlotte sat back, blinking rapidly, more confused than ever. "So, you have not forbidden...people from marrying the ones they love?" she asked, too intimidated to come right out and say Petrus wanted to marry her.

King Milas grinned at her as though he could read her thoughts. "This is a strange and mischievous family, Miss Sloane," he said, "as I'm certain you might have guessed from our unconventional games and rituals. I am not the one who has taken it into his head that duty must be followed above all else. There is another who has convinced himself that self-sacrifice is something a royal must do. It is a silly notion, and no matter how much I argue with him, he has the audacity to tell me how I should be ruling my kingdom and running my family."

The impish light in the king's eyes confused Charlotte even more.

"Won't you please tell me who this is and why you are allowing them to be that way?" she asked.

The king laughed. "Not yet, my dear," he said. "For I believe this lesson will be best learned by taking things further than they should go."

That statement tipped Charlotte over the edge into hopeless confusion. She sighed and slouched a bit. "I do not understand," she said.

"Do not worry on that regard," the king said, taking her hand and patting it. "Simply rest assured knowing that I will not allow the forfeit to continue on to the point where someone will be hurt. I am merely trying to teach someone a lesson."

Charlotte supposed she had to accept that answer, but she most definitely did not like it.

Still, as King Milas got up and begged her pardon before continuing on with whatever duties he had, Charlotte felt as though she were in the middle of a completely foreign situation that she did not know how to get out of. Were Aegirians simply mischievous like that? Or should she be worried about someone other than King Milas throwing a wrench in the works of her love affair with Petrus. And who was the person gumming up the works and standing in the way of everyone's happiness anyhow?

Chapter Eight

C hristmas at the palace of Aegiria was usually frantic, what with all the family traditions Petrus participated in every year. He enjoyed those traditions most of the time, particularly the madness of the family decorating the palace instead of the servants. But everything seemed strained and fraught this year, and as Christmas Eve, the day of the ball, dawned, Petrus was as anxious as he'd ever been.

Everything was about to come to a head. The way his uncle had chided him and Oskar about being true to themselves and true to the family, and about being more considerate toward their guests, who had come a long way to spend the holidays with them, stuck with him. Uncle Milas had been firm and adamant. At the time, Petrus had been certain his uncle meant that he should get on with things, set Charlotte aside, and propose to Lady Jenny, as was always intended.

Now, he wasn't so certain. Uncle Milas had caught him whispering to Charlotte after supper the night before—they'd been debating the wisdom and safety of stealing away up to

Petrus's room to spend the night the way they had several days before—but instead of frowning in disapproval, he'd grinned at Charlotte.

Could it be that Uncle Milas approved of Charlotte after all, and that he might welcome a marriage between them? Charlotte had begun to tell him a story about catching his uncle at the Christmas tree with the boot, but she'd been called away by her friends and by the queen—who wanted to teach them all the dance of the Christmas Princess that would be performed at the ball—and Charlotte had been unable to finish her story.

Everything was a swirl in Petrus's head as he entered the breakfast room on Christmas Eve, anxious for the day to be over so that the many axes that felt as though they were hanging over his head could be banished and everything could be resolved.

One way or another.

"Petrus, there you are." Charlotte half rose from her seat at the breakfast table as Petrus entered the room. She waved him over enthusiastically.

Petrus couldn't help but smile and do as Charlotte commanded, even though her high spirits were completely at odds with his own trepidation.

The table was only sparsely populated at that hour of morning, with most of his family and the guests choosing to take their breakfasts in their rooms. Fredrik and Brigitta were up and seated at the far end of the table, and they eyed Petrus with interest as he took the seat beside Charlotte. Francis and Joseph were seated directly across the table from Charlotte, debating some item in the newspaper that rested between them, which caused Petrus to frown. His conversation with Charlotte would, of necessity, be shallow with such an audience around them instead of allowing the two of them to discuss what they needed to.

Still, Charlotte looked as cheery as a summer daisy as she picked up her teacup and said, "Perhaps now I can tell you about the conversation I had with your uncle the day before yesterday."

Petrus was in the process of reaching for the teapot on the table in front of them and nearly knocked a glass over at the statement. His pulse raced to know what had happened and if it would be of any help with their tangled problems. But he also saw that Francis and Joseph had taken note of the conversation as well. Perhaps a bit too much note.

"Go on, then," he said, grasping the teapot and pretending the subject was casual.

Charlotte smiled at Francis and Joseph as well as at Petrus, letting them know she was aware they were listening. "It was a result of the boot," she said. "The forfeit that I demanded was that he tell me the story of how he met and fell in love with Queen Sylvia."

Petrus's brow shot up in surprise. "And how did he react to that?" He poured himself tea, pretending to be only mildly interested when he was certain that Charlotte had the key to their happily ever after.

Charlotte smiled and continued eating as she told the tale. "They met at a ball in Copenhagen," she said. "He was a student, and she was—well, I suppose she was an attendee. He didn't say why she was there."

She paused to consider, then shook her head. "The point of the matter is that she was a commoner, and that their marriage was not arranged. It was a love match, which he made quite clear."

Hope perked its ears in Petrus's heart. At the same time, Francis and Joseph had been drawn into the story as much as he had.

"So the royal family of Aegiria has a history of love matches?" Francis asked, a little too much sparkle in his eyes as he glanced to Petrus. The two of them had spent a great deal of time together in the last few days, amidst decorating, and Francis knew everything.

"They do," Petrus said carefully, "but I am not sure how far that tradition extends."

Meaning he wasn't certain if he could get away with backing out of a proposed arranged marriage and keep his position with the family intact, considering his birth.

He wasn't certain Charlotte fully grasped the implication, as she continued to smile and eat her eggs on toast. "I think the tradition will extend quite a way," she said. "King Milas seemed to indicate as much to me himself."

She turned to him and smiled as though she had accomplished a coup.

Petrus was at a complete loss. She knew something. Charlotte knew something, and it had bolstered her spirits instead of defeating them. More than anything, Petrus wanted to know what she knew.

But at that very moment, Lady Jenny entered the breakfast room, thus ending all conversation that might resolve things.

"Good morning, Lady Jenny," Petrus greeted her as a woman of her status deserved, standing and bowing to her as he did.

Francis, Joseph, and even Fredrik, who hadn't been involved in the conversation at all, rose to show her a similar sort of respect.

"Good morning, Lady Jenny," Charlotte greeted her in a far cheerier and less formal manner. "Won't you come and sit beside me?"

Petrus's eyes went wide as he took his seat again. He admired Charlotte's ability to befriend anyone, but if things fell apart and he was backed into marrying Lady Jenny for the sake of family duty, she might not wish to be such good friends with the woman.

Perhaps worse still, Lady Jenny was pale and drawn, with dark patches under her eyes, as though she hadn't slept well. Petrus understood. Tomorrow was the day by which her father demanded she be engaged, or else he would take her home.

"Lady Jenny," he began a conversation, not entirely certain what topic would be best at such a fraught breakfast table. "Are you looking forward to the Christmas Eve ball tonight?"

Instead of launching into some sort of effusive excitement about the ball, Lady Jenny's entire countenance seemed to drop. Petrus panicked, wondering how such a simple question could have deflated the woman.

"Petrus!"

Before Petrus could figure out a way to make things right, Oskar appeared in the doorway and called his name. All eyes at the table turned to Oskar—who also looked a little worse for wear. He, too, didn't seem to have slept well, and even though Oskar was normally reserved and dignified, there was a sharper edge of irritation in his voice and his stance.

"Petrus, I must speak with you at once," Oskar said, gesturing for Petrus to come away from the breakfast table.

Petrus blinked, feeling as though he were in the middle of a storm with no idea how he'd gotten there and no idea how to get out. He glanced to Charlotte with a questioning look— and noticed Lady Jenny squeeze her eyes shut and lower her head, sharp blots of pink appearing on her cheeks—then shrugged.

"Go, go," Charlotte said. She wore a frown of the sort she'd worn the other night, when the family had played at solving riddles that the others had come up with.

Petrus nodded, pushed his chair back, wished he was at liberty to kiss Charlotte's forehead, or her lips, before standing all the way and stepping back from the table.

"What is this all about?" he asked Oskar once he met him at the door.

Oskar frowned and glanced back into the breakfast room before heading down the hall.

They didn't go far before Oskar touched his sleeve and drew him into an empty parlor.

"It is Christmas Eve," Oskar said once they'd walked to the far side of the room. Oskar pulled back the curtains to gaze out into the courtyard below. The look on his face was such a tangle of frustration and devastation that it made Petrus squirm.

Petrus waited for him to say something else, to explain the uncomfortable emotion on his face. Emotion was not Petrus's favorite thing to encounter, particularly in another man, his cousin. He would much rather have left Oskar to his own thoughts and feelings, but his cousin had drawn him aside for a reason.

Oskar seemed to tense like a bowstring, then let out a breath all of a sudden and turned to him.

"We all have duties in this family, Petrus. Even you," Oskar said.

At once, Petrus's back went up. Oskar rarely, if ever, held his origin against him, but the comment seemed to be doing just that. It was not the best foot for Oskar to start off on. Petrus did the best he could to tamp down his indignation, but he bristled with offense as Oskar went on.

"We might not like the things we are asked to do on behalf of the kingdom, but it is our duty, as members of the royal family, to comply with the wishes of our king," he said.

"To which duties are you referring?" Petrus asked. He knew, of course. He just wanted Oskar to say it out loud and get to the point.

Oskar huffed through his nose and turned away to the window. He seemed to be gathering his courage as he strode up to Petrus, hands clasped behind his back.

"You know as well as I that the Kingdom of Aegiria holds a precarious place in Europe," he said, sounding very much like the future king he was. "We are a small fish surrounded by sharks in an ever-shrinking pond. It is imperative that we maintain the very best relations with our neighbors, and that we comply to their wishes wherever we can to strengthen alliances."

Petrus clasped his hands behind his back, mimicking Oskar's stance. "You might as well come right out and say it," he said. "Because I already know what you're talking about."

Oskar tensed even more, clenching his jaw for a moment before saying, "Lady Jenny Lindstrom is a marvelous woman, and from the moment she's arrived, you've ignored her."

"I have not ignored her," Petrus argued. "I've been otherwise engaged, searching out and making myself known to my half-brothers."

"Yes, I know," Oskar snapped. "Your *other* family."

Petrus's eyes popped wide. Did Oskar resent his Rathborne-Paxton connections? Was he jealous?

Sure enough, Oskar half turned away and said, "You did not have to run off and disregard the family you already have for a handful of Englishmen."

Surprise was too light a word for everything Petrus felt at those words. "Oskar," he said, leaning toward his cousin, tempted to reach out and touch him. "Just because I have found other blood relations does not make them more important than the family that raised me from birth. I love you all as my very own, and I would never dream of replacing any of you."

"Then why are you defying the wishes of your king to chase after an Englishwoman?" Oskar snapped.

Petrus jerked back, clenching his jaw. Something more was bothering Oskar. The torment in his cousin's eyes went far deeper than the possibility that Petrus might like someone else more than he liked Oskar. That in itself was a rather childish way to think, but Oskar always had had a sentimental heart under his prickly, royal exterior. No one valued the family more than him. Oskar had always taken his duty as the future patriarch, as well as the future king, very, very seriously.

Perhaps that was the matter now.

"It is not merely a matter of duty, Oskar," Petrus explained. "I love Miss Sloane. Surely, love must be accounted for in the execution of family duty as well."

Petrus thought his argument was a good one, but Oskar flinched as though he'd been struck.

"Don't you think I know that?" he hissed. "Love is important. Love is everything. But it is not the only thing."

Petrus's mouth dropped open, and he struggled to follow what Oskar was saying.

Of course, then Oskar flew off on another tangent as he paced away from Petrus and said, "Our alliance with Sweden is crucial to our continued survival, particularly with Germany gaining so much power just to our south." He reached the end of the room, then turned to stride back. "Lord Lindstrom has been specific in the sort of alliance he wants and who he wants it with. His influence with King Oscar is vast. We need that connection."

Petrus didn't disagree with him, but he was at a loss for how to express that. He merely nodded when Oskar reached him again.

"I see," Petrus said when Oskar looked at him as though he demanded an answer.

Oskar seemed to be engaged in some sort of inner conflict, so it was a long time before he paced off in the other direction, saying, "We need an alliance with Germany as well, which is why I will be traveling there in the spring. Princess Feodora—

you remember her from that holiday two years ago—has been suggested as a potential future queen."

Petrus frowned, having a difficult time following Oskar's wild train of thought. "I remember her. Is she not a bit young for you?"

"She will be of a marriageable age soon," Oskar said. "Father doesn't approve, of course."

Petrus shook his head, even more muddled. Oskar seemed to be talking nonsense now. "Why would Uncle Milas not approve of a perfectly fine German princess?"

Oskar had reached the far end of the room and he glanced back, his expression as pinched with emotion as ever. He seemed to balance on the tips of his toes, as if wishing to confess something.

Petrus was growing extraordinarily tired of his cousin's antics. He wanted to get back to Charlotte, wanted to see if they could plot a way to defy his uncle's expectations where Lady Jenny was concerned, but also to discover a way for Lady Jenny to stay in Aegiria against her father's wishes, if that was what she wanted.

Petrus nearly laughed aloud. Fathers and their expectations. He vowed to never be so strict with his own children.

Thoughts of the children he might have with Charlotte softened his irritation a bit, but when Oskar marched back toward him as though the devil were on his heels, Petrus snapped straight.

"Don't you see?" Oskar demanded. "Our lives are not our own. We are the future leaders of this kingdom, and of Europe. We must think strategically, plan carefully, and marry in a manner that best serves Aegiria as a whole."

Something about those words tickled in the back of his mind. It was almost as though Uncle Milas had been arguing against what Oskar was saying when he'd scolded the two of them the other day.

Before Petrus could express those thoughts, Oskar turned his face away and said, "You must marry Lady Jenny to secure the alliance with Sweden, and I must pursue Princess Feodora to secure our place with Germany. It is the only way."

Petrus opened his mouth to protest that it was certainly not the only way, that Oskar never had been very good at plotting strategies, or in changing his mind once he'd made it up, but a flicker of movement near the doorway caught his attention.

"We've been overheard," he said with a sigh, peeling away from Oskar and marching toward the door. He hated the thought that it could have been Charlotte who had overheard him and that she'd taken Oskar's words to mean the two of them couldn't be together.

But Charlotte was far more intelligent than that, which stopped him.

He stepped back to Oskar. "You seem to have your mind made up on this matter, but you have not taken the most important factor into consideration," he said.

"And what factor is that?" Oskar asked, half-mocking.

Oskar's petulant and desperate attitude did not help Petrus approach the situation with the kindness and compassion he knew he should have had. Oskar was thinking as a king only and not as a man, certainly not a man in love.

"I love Charlotte," Petrus said. "That argument alone trumps any attempts at diplomacy and politics that you can come up with. I love her, and while I will do my utmost to make certain things end happily for Lady Jenny, my first loyalty is to love."

"Your duty is to your family and your kingdom," Oskar argued as Petrus marched out to the hall, done with the argument. "Just as mine is. I am sacrificing my heart for Aegiria as well, you know."

Those last words were shouted, but Petrus was no longer in the mood to hear them. His frustration had reached its limit. The Christmas Ball was in a matter of hours, and he was determined to claim the woman he actually loved as his bride, even if it got him thrown out of the family.

Chapter Nine

C harlotte thought nothing of getting up from the breakfast table and following to see where Petrus had gone. She was desperate to talk to him and to tell him what she believed King Milas's words to her the other day meant. She'd tried desperately to tell him before Christmas Eve, but the Aegirian royal family kept themselves and their guests exceptionally busy during the Christmas holidays. They'd toured the city and visited prominent citizens—and common, everyday shops, which Charlotte thought was lovely for royalty—they'd entertained guests and a local children's choir at the palace, and they'd decorated for the ball in every spare moment.

It was a wonder that Charlotte could remember her own name, let alone find time to share her thoughts with Petrus. But now was the time. Even though it meant leaving the breakfast room just as Priya was arriving—she truly would have enjoyed telling the whole saga to her friend—if there was even a slight possibility that Charlotte could catch Petrus before he was dragged off into more holiday preparations, she would take it.

And besides, she'd been able to leave poor, distraught Lady Jenny in Ellen's capable, American hands. No one could withstand the gregariousness of Ellen Rathborne-Paxton, once she decided she wanted to talk to you.

Charlotte was surprised that she didn't have to go far before she heard the sound of Petrus's voice. He and Prince Oskar must have secluded themselves in one of the parlors not far from the breakfast room, but out of the way of foot traffic.

At first, she approached the door at her usual pace, a smile on her face and a spring in her step. But as Prince Oskar raised his voice, as she heard the angst of his words, Charlotte slowed her steps. Instead of bursting into the room and interrupting the men, which could embarrass them, she crept up to the side of the door and leaned carefully so that she could listen without being observed.

"Don't you see? Our lives are not our own. We are the future leaders of this kingdom, and of Europe. We must think strategically, plan carefully, and marry in a manner that best serves Aegiria as a whole."

Charlotte caught her breath and pressed a hand to her stomach at those words. They expressed the very sentiment that she had been trying to avoid thinking about for days. Crown Prince Oskar might just have the right of it. Despite all his romantic words and kisses, Petrus might not be at liberty to marry where he pleased.

As soon as that thought struck her, she lowered her shoulders, shook her head, and nearly blew a raspberry at herself to express how ridiculous the idea was. Hadn't King Milas just told her that he was less concerned with diplomacy than with his family being happy?

Another thought struck her as the conversation went on. Perhaps Prince Oskar didn't know his father's mind. Perhaps the ideas he was expressing to Petrus were his own and not King Milas's at all.

Charlotte sucked in a breath and stood a bit taller. But, of course, that was it. King Milas had said that the pressure to marry for the sake of alliance had not come from him, it was coming from someone else. That someone else must have been Crown Prince Oskar.

As if to prove her new theory, she heard Prince Oskar say, "Your duty is to your family and your kingdom. Just as mine is. I am sacrificing my heart for Aegiria as well, you know."

Charlotte nearly jumped for joy as all the pieces suddenly fit into place in her mind.

Unfortunately, her enthusiasm at discovering the truth also meant she gave her hiding place away. The conversation stopped, and she was certain Petrus and Oskar turned toward the door.

Charlotte ran before she could think better of it. She dashed away, embarrassed at being caught eavesdropping on princes, and ducked around the nearest corner she could find.

That corner turned out to lead her into a servants' corridor. She hurried along until the corridor made a turn, but once she was beyond that, well out of sight of Petrus and Prince Oskar, even if they should come after her, she stopped.

With a huff for herself, Charlotte said, "Why are you running, you ninny?" She continued in her mind, wondering what was the point of running away from Petrus when she could speak to him directly and sort the whole thing out.

She had just decided to turn and march back to the parlor so that she might confront Petrus and Prince Oskar and tell them she had the entire muddle sorted, when a maid stepped out of a room to one side carrying the most beautiful garland of flowers and candles Charlotte had ever seen.

"What is that?" she asked, pressing a hand to her heart and stepping forward to get a closer look at the wonder.

"If you please, Miss Sloane," the maid said with a proud

smile, her round cheeks pink, "it's the crown for the Christmas Princess."

Charlotte made a sound of wonder as the maid held the crown out so Charlotte could get a better look. It was a simple circlet of holy, ivy, and pine with turquoise and green ribbon woven throughout. There were also jewels, Charlotte noted, and once the long, white candles were lit, the whole thing would glitter magically.

"It must be terribly unsettling to wear lit candles in one's hair," she said, reaching out to touch one of the candles, but pulling back before she did.

The maid laughed. "That's why the Christmas Princess is chosen a few hours in advance, so she can take care not to puff her hair up with false rolls or to use any substance that might ignite to style her hair. It's also why the chosen woman is given a cap that repulses flame to wear under the crown."

The maid's words sent a stir through Charlotte's gut, but not for the reason she would have thought.

"Do you know who has been chosen to be the Christmas Princess, then?" she asked.

The maid lost her smile and heaved a small sigh. "It was to be Lady Jenny, of course," she said. "Everyone in the palace has expected that Prince Petrus would propose to her by now." The maid suddenly seemed to realize whom she was talking to and blinked rapidly, her face going even redder. "Begging your pardon, that is, miss."

"Oh, I understand the situation full well," Charlotte said, waving off the maid's slip. An idea struck her, and she smiled even wider. "Does Lady Jenny know she is to be the Christmas Princess?" she asked.

The maid looked sheepish for a moment. She glanced up and down the hall before saying. "She has known for weeks now. Several people in the palace know. None of us are certain what will happen, now that, well, now that you are here, Miss Sloane."

Charlotte continued to smile, even though, by all outward appearances, the entire Christmas Princess tradition was in danger. But after what she'd just overheard in the parlor, she was certain she could set things to right.

"Proceed as intended," she said, patting the maid's arm. "I must find Lady Jenny and get to the bottom of this muddle."

"Yes, miss," the maid said, seemingly both confused and fascinated by Charlotte's sudden air of authority.

Charlotte could, indeed, be an authority when she needed to be. If she had her way, the palace staff might see her as something of an authority for a while to come.

She wound her way through the maze of the servants' hallways, coming out at a part of the palace that she didn't expect. For a moment she stood in the ornate hall, debating whether to search for Petrus to share her new theory with him and to let him in on the plan she was fomenting, or to find Lady Jenny first so that she might pry a confession from the woman.

Fate decided for her when she spotted Lady Jenny hurrying down the corridor where she stood, looking suspicious. She clutched something to her stomach that caught a bit of light and flashed.

A broad smile split Charlotte's face and she ran after Lady Jenny, knowing full well she was going to the library. Sure enough, just as Charlotte skidded to a stop in front of the library door, Lady Jenny was reaching out toward the tree, the hideous boot in her hand.

"Ah ha!" Charlotte stopped her, stepping into the room.

Lady Jenny jumped and squealed, then finished hanging the boot. She whipped to face Charlotte once she did, her eyes round. "You've caught me," she said, looking as though she meant it in more ways than applied to a silly Christmas tradition.

Charlotte eased up her stance and walked fully into the room. She reached for Lady Jenny's hand, saying, "Now you must do something for me as a forfeit."

Reluctantly, Lady Jenny took the offered hand and allowed herself to be led to the couch. As the two of them sat, she said, "What do you want from me?"

The way she asked the question made Charlotte wonder if the woman expected her to shout and rail, or even beat her.

Instead, Charlotte said, "I want you to tell me the truth."

Lady Jenny swallowed. "The truth?"

Charlotte was nearly too excited to reveal all to maintain her composure. "I would like you to tell me how long you and Crown Prince Oskar have been in love."

Lady Jenny sucked in a breath, then burst into tears. The transformation from timid and sad to limp and sobbing was so fast that Charlotte knew her theory was correct. She could do nothing then but scoot closer to the woman and draw her into her arms as if they'd been friends for a decade.

"I love him so," Lady Jenny sniffled. "I have almost from the start. Prince Petrus is a very nice man, but he has been in Aegiria so little since my arrival, and Oskar was so kind as to entertain me in his cousin's absence."

Everything became so much clearer to Charlotte. "The man you were sent to charm was off losing his heart to someone else," she said, unable to stop herself from smiling. "And the one you were never meant to notice or be noticed by became your whole world."

"Yes," Lady Jenny said, straightening and staring at Charlotte with a look of wonder and gratitude. That look stiffened to worry, though. "You...you are not angry with me?"

Charlotte laughed and rubbed Lady Jenny's back. "Why should I be angry with you? The man I love loves me in return. And if what I just overheard is true, the man you love adores you just as much."

But instead of being heartened by those words, Lady Jenny burst into tears once more. "Oskar does love me, but he says he must marry someone else, a German princess. He says that he cannot let his heart rule him, he must rise to the needs of his kingdom and do what is right for Aegiria."

"Nonsense," Charlotte said, still rubbing Lady Jenny's back. "I do not know Prince Oskar well, but it seems to me as though he is taking his duty as the future king a bit too seriously."

"Oskar is a very serious man," Lady Jenny agreed wetly, nodding and forcing herself to sit straight. "I...." She sent Charlotte a sheepish look. "I believe he has read a few too many novels about heroes of old who sacrifice themselves for the greater good."

Again, Charlotte laughed. "And they say that we are the weaker sex, that we are the ones prone to flights of fancy and imagination." She shook her head. "Men are just as bad, if not worse. If they conjure up a way they think they can become a proud and tragically noble hero, they'll snatch at it without trying to find another solution."

"Yes, Oskar is a very proud man," Lady Jenny said. "Just the other night, I tried to tell him—"

She stopped, her face going redder than Charlotte thought anyone's face could go.

A moment later, Charlotte put the pieces together. Her eyes went wide, and she grinned from ear to ear. "You spent the night with Prince Oskar, didn't you?" she asked.

Lady Jenny's expression went from shocked and horrified to pinched and guilty. She lowered her head and said, "You must think I am the lowest sort of strumpet."

"Quite the contrary," Charlotte said, unexpected joy and a sense of closeness to Lady Jenny filling her. When Lady Jenny glanced up at her in question, she leaned close and whispered,

"I spent the night in Petrus's bed the night of Huckle Buckle Beanstalk."

Lady Jenny gasped and sat straighter, blinking her tear-wet lashes at Charlotte in surprise. "That is the night I slept in Oskar's bed."

It was all Charlotte could do not to giggle like a fiend. "I'd wager the two of you did more than sleeping," she said, as if she and Lady Jenny were wenches at the tavern her oldest brother favored in Brighton.

Lady Jenny laughed so unexpectedly that she snorted. That made both of them laugh hard, covering their mouths and sagging together as their friendship blossomed and bound them together.

But after the laughter, Lady Janny moaned. "What are we to do?" she asked. "Oskar is so determined that I should marry Petrus to secure an alliance between Aegiria and Sweden, and he is intent on courting Princes Feodora to bolster relations between Aegiria and Germany."

"Prince Oskar is wrong," Charlotte said bluntly. "He is behaving as a typical man and thinking too much where he should be feeling. Even King Milas thinks so, or so I believe."

"Truly?" That seemed to raise Lady Jenny's spirits higher than ever.

"He said something to me the other day that led me to believe he does not approve of his son sacrificing love for duty." Charlotte blinked, slouching a bit as all the facets of the problem presented itself to her. "Why does the king not simply tell Prince Oskar that he's being an arse and that he should marry you?"

"Oh, but he *has* told him," Lady Jenny said. When Charlotte turned to her in surprise, she went on with, "That was the reason the king took Oskar and Prince Petrus to task the other day. He's told Oskar on more than one occasion that love is more important than duty."

It was like someone had lit a torch to illuminate all. The conversation she and Petrus had overheard while hiding in the closet in the library was not about Oskar's duty to marry for diplomacy, it was about his duty to marry for love and to set that example to the people of Aegiria.

"And what did Oskar say to that?" Charlotte asked.

Lady Jenny huffed. "He said that his father had gone soft and was underestimating the situation." She paused, then asked, "Why are young men such dolts when they are of a certain age?"

"Because they grow full of themselves before they grow sense," Charlotte answered, shaking her head. "My brother Benjamin is an absolute pill when he gets it into his head that just because he has reached the venerable age of twenty, he knows more than Papa."

Lady Jenny laughed, then covered her mouth with her hand, as if that was the wrong reaction.

A moment later, she drooped again.

"What do we do?" she asked. "What is obvious to us isn't obvious to Oskar at all. How can we overcome his pride to show him that he and I belong together, as do you and Prince Petrus?"

Charlotte smiled. This was the moment she'd hoped they were leading up to. "I have a plan," she said.

"Oh, thank God," Lady Jenny sighed, clasping her hands to her heart. "Whatever it is, I will help you. I will do whatever I must to convince Oskar that he, too, deserves love, and that duty will take care of itself."

"Very well said." Charlotte smiled, then scooted closer to Lady Jenny. "Now, this is my plan, and it involves the ball tonight and the revelation of the Christmas princess."

She grasped Lady Jenny's hands and spilled out the entire plan to her, giddy at heart and knowing the two of them were about to give Aegiria a Christmas it wouldn't soon forget.

Chapter Ten

Petrus had left the parlor where he and Oskar had argued intent on finding Charlotte and pouring his heart out to her. He'd been foolish not to simply make a declaration to her and to his family that he loved her and would marry her no matter what anyone else thought.

But she was no longer in the breakfast room when he returned there, and a quick search of all the places he thought Charlotte could be turned up empty. Before he could search much farther, his mother caught him in the hall and dragged him off to help with some of the frantic, last-minute preparations for inviting the people of Aegiria into the palace for the ball.

"I must warn you, Petrus," she said as she took him up to their family's wing of the palace to change into more formal attire, "that a rumor has begun circulating that tonight's Christmas Princess is to be your bride."

"Is that what people think?" he asked, uncertain whether he felt horrified or amused by the rumor. He supposed that all depended on who the Christmas Princess was.

"It is," his mother said. "And it is the talk of the town, of the entire kingdom. Even more people than usual applied to be let into the palace for the ball to see the unveiling, and for the first time, the royal family might have to turn some of our people away."

Petrus was stunned by the news. He'd had no idea that the people of Aegiria cared so much about the royal family.

No, that wasn't true. He had no idea that the people cared so much about *him*. He was the odd one out, the one everyone knew was secretly a bastard, albeit one whom the royal family had embraced. But as touching as it was to hear that the people of his kingdom cared about him, it still sent prickles down his neck.

"Do they think Lady Jenny is to be the Christmas Princess and my bride?" he asked his mother as they reached their private quarters.

His mother simply hummed and sent him a knowing sideways look.

They did think that. His mother's lack of an answer was answer enough. It made Petrus want to find Charlotte to explain more than ever. He rushed through the process of dressing in a festive suit with accents of turquoise and green, the official colors of Aegiria, which represented the sea and the island. He didn't care how handsome he looked or how impressed the public might be with his appearance, he merely wanted to find Charlotte.

But still, when he came down to search the palace after changing, he could not find her. Activity at the palace had reached its height, so no one was able to stop and help him search, or tell him where they had last seen her either.

It was mildly concerning in the morning. It was worrying when Charlotte didn't appear for luncheon with the rest of the family—although only half the family managed to stop by the dining room to eat anyhow. Even Lady Jenny was missing from the meal. Petrus's anxiety became full-blown in the afternoon when Charlotte was still nowhere to be found.

He was certain she would have turned up for supper, but there was no formal supper for the family that night. The palace doors were opened for the ball just as the sun went down, which was quite early. The candles were all lit, the decorations they'd taken so much time and effort to hang sparkled in the winter light, and the stream of citizens from Aegiria, all carrying their bundles of woven wheat and greenery to give to the Christmas Princess, filtered into the palace.

"Where is Charlotte?" Petrus wondered aloud after searching most of the ground floor and eventually ending up in the ballroom as it filled with noise and heat and festively dressed people.

He'd moved to stand near Francis, who was speaking with Oskar on the corner of the dais at the far end of the ballroom.

"You've lost track of her, then?" Francis asked, his joy and excitement a contrast to Petrus's worry. And Oskar's sourness on top of that.

"I haven't seen her since breakfast," Petrus said. He would have scrubbed his hands through his hair in frustration if he didn't think his mother would take him to task for mussing up a perfectly arranged hairstyle, no matter how old he was.

"Perhaps you should be less concerned about Miss Sloane's whereabouts and more concerned about Lady Jenny's," Oskar said in a tight voice, searching the ballroom instead of looking at Petrus.

Everything he and Oskar had discussed that morning came rushing back to him. He didn't agree with Oskar's insistence on self-sacrifice for the good of the family, and the time had come to say something about it.

"Oskar, I know you care about this family and Aegiria more than anything in the world," he began as more of the family headed toward the dais. It was a signal that the revelation of the Christmas Princess would happen soon.

Before Petrus could go on, Oskar turned sharply to him, leaned in as if conscious they were being watched, and hissed, "There are things that I care about more than this family and Aegiria."

Petrus snapped his mouth shut and stared at his cousin with wide eyes. The news came as a complete shock to him. He couldn't imagine what on earth his overly serious cousin could love more than—

It hit him so hard it knocked the air from his lungs.

"You love her," he said, lowering his voice to the point where he could barely be heard over the low din of the ball's guests. "You love Lady Jenny."

Oskar flushed dark and turned his head away. To anyone else, it would look like he was staring out over his future subjects, his back stiff and his shoulders squared. His chin was raised as well, giving him a look of power. But Petrus knew him too well, knew that the emotion in Oskar's eyes was misery and not aloof pride in his people.

"I do," he admitted before peeking back at Petrus.

Absolutely everything fell into place—the way Oskar had been advocating for Lady Jenny for weeks now, the way they sat close to each other while deliberately not looking at each other, the way Oskar seemed to soften when he was around Lady Jenny. Even stumbling across Lady Jenny coming out of the family wing of the palace early the other morning took on a whole new significance.

"How did this happen?" Petrus asked, though it wasn't quite what he wanted to say.

Oskar let out a breath—one it seemed he had been holding for months—and faced Petrus with more honesty than he had in ages. "Jenny was sent here to marry into the royal family, to marry you," he said. "The match was meant to bind Aegiria and Sweden closer together, just as I have said all along. But you were off in England for so much of the summer. Someone needed to entertain Jenny to stop her from feeling cast off."

Part of Petrus felt guilty for causing Lady Jenny distress, but if he had stayed in Aegiria and wooed her, he never would have found his half-brothers, or Charlotte.

"We found that we were quite suited to each other right from the start," Oskar went on. "We share a fondness for the same books and for...well, for fishing, if you must know."

Petrus burst into a smile despite himself. "You and Lady Jenny went fishing together?" The idea of two such serious people sitting in a boat, dangling fishing lines over the water was almost comical.

"Yes," Oskar said, frowning as if Petrus were making fun of him. "We enjoy each other's company."

So many things made sense. "She loves you too," Petrus said. "That's why she's been so miserable this last week. She hasn't been upset because I've been dragging my heels proposing to her, she's merely terrified that I might *actually* propose. Then she would feel obligated to accept. But it is you she truly wishes to be with."

"I...I believe so," Oskar said, hanging his head.

Even more things made sense. Uncle Milas's admonition to the two of them the other day, for example. And Oskar's frustrated statement that he was sacrificing love too.

"Then dammit, man," Petrus said, taking a step closer to Oskar as the dais became crowded with family and a veritable horde of Aegirian citizens flowed into the room. "Why have you not proposed to Lady Jenny? Surely, it would be an even larger diplomatic coup for Lord Lindstrom's daughter to marry the crown prince of Aegiria instead of a dubious cousin."

Oskar glared at Petrus, but Petrus could see there was more heartbreak than true anger in his eyes.

"It is necessary that I marry a German princess," Oskar insisted. "Germany is far more dangerous than Sweden. They present more of a threat to Aegiria than Sweden ever could. It is absolutely vital that I marry a German to secure an alliance."

Petrus shook his head and rubbed a hand over his face. Oskar was good and noble and cared so deeply for Aegiria, but he was being a rank idiot.

"Oskar, you have six younger siblings. And there's Frederik and Briggita too," Petrus argued. "That's eight more chances for Aegiria to secure the all-important alliance with Germany through a royal marriage. And that's only counting your family and mine. We have more cousins out there, you and I. You do not have to take all of this onto your own shoulders."

"But I am the crown prince," Oskar argued, his emotions close to bursting and his youth showing through. "I have a duty to my kingdom."

"And would that duty not be best served by marrying the woman you love and showing our people what true happiness and wedded bliss looks like?" Petrus asked. Which was exactly what Uncle Milas had been arguing the day he and Charlotte had overheard from the library closet. "We could both show them, you and I. We could both marry the women we love."

"I—"

Oskar seemed at a complete loss. He wasn't given a chance to sort out his thoughts—which Petrus could see full well were tumultuous. The king and queen had made their grand entrance into the ballroom and had just stepped up onto the stage.

Everyone in the packed ballroom fell into a hush as the king raised his hands.

"Ladies and gentlemen, beloved subjects and guests," the king began. "I give you my wife, the indomitable Queen Sylvia."

The king gestured to the queen as the ballroom erupted into applause.

Queen Sylvia stepped forward, radiant in Aegirian turquoise and green, the gems of her crown and jewelry sparkling, and gestured for the people to be quiet.

"My husband and I thank you all for joining us this Christmas Eve in celebration of our kingdom, our family, and our Savior's birth," she began. "As you know, it is our tradition that every Christmas Eve, a Christmas Princess is crowned to represent the love we have for each other and for you. In the past, this princess has been the chosen bride of a member of the royal family. It has been quite a long time since any members of the family have been of an age where this tradition can be carried out, but tonight, once again, to our great delight, the Christmas Princess will be the bride of a prince."

The crowd gasped and murmured with excitement and joy.

Petrus's stomach twisted into knots. He had the horrible feeling that he was about to be trapped into proposing to Lady Jenny in front of half the kingdom of Aegiria. If that were the case, there was no way he would be able to choose Charlotte as his own, or to let Oskar have the woman he loved.

He had to do something. He cleared his throat and stepped closer to the center of the dais, where the king and queen stood.

It was the wrong move.

"And here is our royal groom," Queen Sylvia said, gesturing to Petrus as though he'd stepped forward on queue. "Prince Petrus."

The crowd gasped and applauded, their eyes bright, excitement humming in the air.

Petrus was worried he might be sick. He smiled at the crowd, but lost that smile when he reached his aunt and uncle at the center of the dais.

"I'm not certain this is the best—" he began.

He was cut short as the double doors at the far end of the ballroom opened to reveal the Christmas Princess. There was a rush of rustling skirts and shifting bodies as everyone turned and stepped aside to see who it was. They created an aisle from the back doorway to the dais as they did.

There was a second gasp of shock as not one, but two women appeared in the doorway. Petrus's jaw dropped as well as both Charlotte and Lady Jenny stepped into the light of the ballroom, holding the Christmas Princess's crown between them. They were dressed in identical red dresses—although how the two of them had managed to obtain two of the same gown on such short notice was a mystery to Petrus.

That mystery could wait for another day. As Charlotte and Lady Jenny stepped forward, walking through the ballroom and approaching the dais with uncertain smiles, everyone watched, holding their breath. Petrus was vaguely aware of Oskar moving up to his side. The two of them watched the women come closer, and Petrus thought he might die with the suspense of the whole thing.

"I don't understand," someone in the front of the crowd, one of the Aegirian nobles, said. "Is Prince Petrus going to marry two women at once?"

"Aegiria might be progressive," someone else said, "but we're not *that* progressive."

Charlotte and Lady Jenny stepped up onto the dais and stood so that they faced Petrus and Oskar, the king and queen standing between them. Charlotte wore a look of delicious mischief, which let Petrus know at once that the entire thing had been her idea. Lady Jenny looked completely terrified and appealed to Oskar with her eyes for help.

A long, tense silence followed before the king said, "It appears as though we may have two brides before us." He stared hard at his son, as if telling him the time had come to step up and do the right thing.

Oskar practically vibrated with stress before it all seemed to evaporate around him. He dropped his shoulders and let himself smile. It was the first smile Petrus had seen from his cousin in weeks.

"Yes, we do," he said in answer to his father's words. He stepped forward, his eyes fixed on Lady Jenny, and offered her his hand. "Jenny, I love you more than I ever thought it was possible to love anything. You are my sun and my moon, my spring flower and my autumn leaves. I have tried so hard to do what is right for my family and my kingdom, but I see now that the right thing is to love and to show that love in all its glory. Will you be not only my Christmas Princess but my bride and the joy of my heart?"

Everyone in the room held their breath. Even Petrus felt the romance of the moment.

Lady Jenny let go of her side of the Christmas Princess's crown, which Charlotte scrambled to catch with her other hand to keep it from spilling to the ground and its candles from igniting something. She stepped toward Oskar, taking both his hands as he offered them.

"Yes," she said, and even though her voice was tiny and quiet, it seemed to ring throughout the ballroom. "Yes, Oskar, I will marry you. I love you."

"My darling," Oskar said, and then, in front of everyone, he pulled Jenny into his arms for a kiss.

The crowded ballroom erupted with cheers and shouts of approval. The king and queen beamed to show that they approved of the match as well. Not a single person in the crowd paused to wonder why Crown Prince Oskar was the one who had just become engaged in front of them when the queen had stated that Prince Petrus was the one to become a groom. They likely all thought it was just another Aegirian royal family Christmas prank, although some of them might have guessed the truth when Charlotte stepped forward to affix the Christmas Princess's crown on Lady Jenny's head, with Petrus's help, and then moved back to hold Petrus's hand, the two of them beaming at each other, as they watched Oskar and Lady Jenny wave to the room.

"I wasn't certain how that was going to go," Charlotte told Petrus with a laugh about fifteen minutes later, after the ceremony was over and the dancing had begun.

Petrus held Charlotte in his arms, beaming happily at her as they whirled around the ballroom in a waltz. "I think it went splendidly," he said, so proud of Charlotte that he could burst.

"We only had today to plan," Charlotte confessed. "Lady Jenny only confessed to me that she loved Prince Oskar this morning. We talked about it and worked things out, and agreed that we should both appear as the Christmas Princess and force the two of you to choose who would marry who."

Petrus arched one eyebrow. "How did you know I would not choose Lady Jenny, as I was supposed to?"

Charlotte threw back her head and laughed. It was the jolliest sound Petrus had ever heard, and it made him feel warm, inside and out.

"Dear Petrus," she said, shaking her head at him, heat and naughtiness in her beautiful eyes. "You would never choose Lady Jenny, as marvelous as she is, over me. You love me, and you are a man of honor."

"Precisely," Petrus said, agreeing with her, but enjoying the teasing. "Which is why I could have done my duty, as Oskar wanted me to, and married Lady Jenny to secure that alliance."

Charlotte wasn't fooled for a moment. She continued to shake her head as they whirled around the room and looked at him as if he were her own, dearest fool. "You've already compromised me," she said. "And while I would never, ever hold that against you and use it to force you into a marriage, I know full well that you are not the sort to take that action lightly."

"Neither are you," Petrus said, more in love with Charlotte than ever for her honestly and bluntness.

The whole thing was wonderful, but Petrus was still left feeling as though something was unfinished.

When the orchestra finished the song and the swirling couples stepped apart to applaud, then move to the sides of the room to find new partners for the next dance, Petrus grasped Charlotte's hand and swept her all the way out of the room. There was too much activity for anyone to notice them leaving the ball and hurrying down the hallway like children to one of the servants' stairways.

"Where are we going?" Charlotte asked as they slipped into the narrow passage and made their way up.

"My darling, I think you know full well where we are going," Petrus said with a sly, sideways look.

Charlotte giggled, proving that she knew as well as he did.

They stepped out of the servants' stairs on the second floor, then rushed along the hallway hand in hand until they crossed all the way to the other side of the palace and the family wing. No one was there to see Petrus tug Charlotte into his apartment, or to scold him for locking the door behind them and closing his arms around her for a passionate kiss.

"You are my own true princess," Petrus said as he kissed her, letting his heart have free reign. "The story of tonight might be Oskar's and Lady Jenny's story, but they will write ballads of our love someday as well."

Charlotte laughed as she kissed him back, standing on her toes so that she could throw her arms around his shoulders and meet his passion with fervor of her own. "Our story will be far less suitable for public audience," she said, inching back and gazing up at him with invitation in her eyes.

Petrus laughed and set to work straight away unbuttoning his formal jacket as he moved toward the bedroom.

They both hurried out of their clothes—as much as one could hurry out of formal ball attire—as they made it to the bedroom. With the pulse of passion beating furiously, they helped each other undress, pausing for kisses now and then, until they were able to tumble into bed and tangle up in each other's limbs and heat.

Charlotte was delightful in every way, but the way she caressed and embraced him, as though they had been lovers for years instead of days, filled him with a sense of pride and responsibility for her happiness and her pleasure. He kissed and stroked every bit of her that he could reach, listening for her sighs and feeling her body tense and shiver to know whether he was giving her everything she wanted.

But just as he reached the point where he couldn't hold himself back any longer, he paused, balancing himself above her and gazing down at her wanton beauty.

"Charlotte, my angel," he said, breathless and aroused by her restlessness. "Even though we aren't in front of an audience and I've no words to make a grandiloquent speech, will you marry me?"

Charlotte sucked in a breath, and Petrus was certain he could feel the bolt of excitement that passed through her. "Yes!" she said, reaching up to grasp the sides of his face. "Yes, oh, yes! I was about to propose to you myself, in fact."

That made Petrus laugh. It was so like Charlotte to take charge of things, whether it was right and proper or not, when they needed taking charge of. He loved that about her. He loved everything about her.

"I love you," he told her as he adjusted their bodies so that they would fit together, then sank himself deep into her heat. Charlotte moaned with pleasure and arched to meet him, which only encouraged him. "I love you with everything I am and everything I ever will be," he said, feeling his control dissolve as he melded with her.

"I love you too, Petrus," she gasped, then let out a quick, "Oh!" as he plunged into her over and over.

Part of him felt he should have prolonged their love-making and given her all the pleasure she could have asked for and more. There would be time for that later. They would have their whole lives to please and delight each other, and he was certain they would. For now, Petrus just wanted to be one with the woman he loved more than anything. And from the way she met his thrusts and clung to him, digging her finger-tips into the flesh of his back, that was what she wanted too.

He was surprised when Charlotte tilted her head back and let out an impassioned cry as her body convulsed around him. She was so free with her pleasure that she'd managed to reach her climax despite his too-hasty lovemaking. It was a joy to watch and to feel, and he let himself go and spill into her with abandon. They were one, together for the rest of their lives.

"I love you, my darling," he said again as they came down from the high of the moment, snuggling together. "I love you so much."

"And I love you," Charlotte replied, a happy hum in her voice that Petrus was determined to keep there forever.

I hope you have enjoyed Charlotte and Petrus's story! They are such a fun couple, and they were a joy to write.

A few things of note... I've included two things in this story that are real-life traditions from my family. THE BOOT really does exist! It was given to my brother for Christmas when we were kids, and yes, it is every bit as hideous as I've described it. And my brother would always hang it front and center on the tree...and I would come along and move it to the back of the tree. Over and over. I've expanded the game in this book, but the heart of the tradition remains. I still own the boot, even though my brother and I haven't lived together for decades, and I still hang it...on the BACK of the Christmas tree.

Huckle Buckle Beanstalk is a family game too, and it's a lot of fun! The ivory Chinese man really exists too, but like I said in the story, you can play it with any object. I love to play Huckle Buckle Beanstalk with my niece and nephew (though it works best in a large group), and we tend to use Lego figures as the Huckle Buckle. It's a fun, low-maintenance party game!

And while this might be the last book in *The Unsuitable Brides* series, it's just the beginning of a new series, *The Aegirian Royals*! There are seven other young royals to marry off, after all. And it really would be good for Aegiria to have that alliance with Germany. So look for *The Aegirian Royals* in the new year! And be sure to sign up for my newsletter so that you're informed when the new series begins! Sign up here: http://eepurl.com/cbaVMH

If you enjoyed this book and would like to hear more from me, please sign up for my newsletter! When you sign up, you'll get a free, full-length novella, *A Passionate Deception*. Victorian identity theft has never been so exciting in this story of hope, tricks, and starting over. Part of my West Meets East series, *A Passionate Deception* can be read as a stand-alone. Pick up your free copy today by signing up to receive my newsletter (which I only send out when I have a new release)!

Sign up here: http://eepurl.com/cbaVMH

Are you on social media? I am! Come and join the fun on Facebook: http://www.facebook.com/merryfarmerreaders

. . .

I'm also a huge fan of Instagram and post lots of original content there: https://www.instagram.com/merryfarmer/

ONE LAST THING! Do you crave historical romance filled with passion and red-hot chemistry? Come join me and my author friends in the Facebook group, Historical Harlots, for exclusive giveaways, chat with amazing HistRom authors, raunchy shenanigans, and more!

https://www.facebook.com/groups/2102138599813601

About the Author

I hope you have enjoyed *Have Yourself a Merry Little Christmas*. If you'd like to be the first to learn about when new books in the series come out and more, please sign up for my newsletter here: http://eepurl.com/cbaVMH And remember, Read it, Review it, Share it! For a complete list of works by Merry Farmer with links, please visit http://wp.me/P5ttjb-14F.

USA Today Bestselling Author Merry Farmer is an award-winning novelist who lives in suburban Philadelphia with her cats, Peter and Justine. She has been writing since she was ten years old and realized one day that she didn't have to wait for the teacher to assign a creative writing project to write something. It was the best day of her life. She then went on to earn not one but two degrees in History so that she would always have something to write about. Her books have reached the Top 100 at Amazon, iBooks, and Barnes & Noble, and have been named finalists in the prestigious RONE and Rom Com Reader's Crown awards.

Acknowledgments

I owe a huge debt of gratitude to my awesome beta-readers, Caroline Lee and Jolene Stewart, for their suggestions and advice. And double thanks to Julie Tague, for being a truly excellent editor and to Cindy Jackson for being an awesome assistant!

Click here for a complete list of other works by Merry Farmer.

Printed in Great Britain
by Amazon